SA
P

MOVING ON

Hailey had prepared her younger sister, Kate, for a life at university; a brighter future than her own. But then Kate falls in love with an older man, David, suddenly leaving Hailey free. Meanwhile James, a successful, wealthy but unfulfilled PR Manager, finds his plans foiled when an accident causes him to miss his flight . . . and one kind act surprisingly leads to another . . . Both Hailey and James' lives change as they move on and in the process they discover love.

VALERIE HOLMES

MOVING ON

Complete and Unabridged

LINFORD
Leicester

First published in Great Britain in 2010

First Linford Edition
published 2010

British Library CIP Data

Holmes, Valerie.
  Moving on. - - (Linford romance library)
  1. Love stories.
  2. Large type books.
  I. Title II. Series
  823.9'2–dc22

ISBN 978–1–44480–108–8

Published by
F. A. Thorpe (Publishing)
Anstey, Leicestershire

Set by Words & Graphics Ltd.
Anstey, Leicestershire
Printed and bound in Great Britain by
T. J. International Ltd., Padstow, Cornwall

This book is printed on acid-free paper

1

Hailey picked up the letter that had been delivered early that morning. It was addressed to Kate and it looked official.

'Kate, I think this may be your offer of a place at university.' Hailey almost ran into her younger sister as she emerged from the living room doorway.

Kate took the letter out of her sister's hand and opened it. 'Yes, you're right, it is.' Kate casually walked into the living room and dropped the letter on the table.

Hailey retrieved it, stunned by her sister's attitude. 'What are you doing, Kate? It's your place. It's what you want. Why throw it away?'

'Because, it isn't what I want. Not anymore; I've changed my mind. I've decided to take a job instead.' Kate turned around and faced Hailey.

'But what about going to university, Kate?' Hailey looked at her younger sister in disbelief. 'You surely can't be serious about this.' She was almost shaking, an unusual reaction for Hailey who was usually calm and understanding. She could tell her protestations were having little if no impact on Kate's determined stance. She was as stubborn as a mule, and Hailey thought, at times, about as intelligent. Determined to dissuade her at all costs, Hailey continued undaunted.

'The jobs around here don't pay that well unless you have qualifications. Kate, get your degree then you can go anywhere and be anything you want to be. Don't throw your opportunity away. Why give up now?' Hailey tried to sound calm but it was proving difficult.

'I shan't be taking a job locally. I've decided to make a clean break, Hailey; I'm going to work in London.' Kate patted her sister's back as she looked totally stunned. 'Sorry for dropping it on you like this. I've been waiting for the right time to tell you for a while, but I guess this is as good as it is going to get.'

Hailey forced herself to speak. 'London's a huge, impersonal city. You don't know anyone there. It's expensive and getting more so by the day. How will you survive there and pay for yourself? Think, Kate, this isn't something you can decide to do without months of planning! It is your future you are messing up. Look, try going to university. We can get grants or student loans for that. Don't worry, we'll manage. If it doesn't work out then take a gap year. Many students do, but at least give it a go, Kate.'

Kate just stood there, arms folded. 'Yes, you're right. I agree with you completely. It is my life and my future — as in, not yours, Hailey.' She smiled back which provoked a reaction of growing anger within her sister. This was one argument she could not win, so why, she asked herself, was she trying so hard to? The answer was both simple and complex. Simple because she loved Kate and complex because she envied her for taking this brave, stupid and life-changing decision.

'I can't believe you're even considering it. Have you completely lost your mind? Where will you live, Kate?' Hailey was almost at the point of giving in, backing off and letting her do what she wanted. A daunting thought struck her — she too would be able to focus on her own life instead of always considering Kate's future.

Kate yawned in an exaggerated, bored manner and looked away. 'Come on, Hailey. If you'd had the chance to go off and live a life, wouldn't you have grabbed it with both hands?'

'No, Kate, not like this! I always wanted to go university to study history or art but I've never had the chance — you have.' Hailey tried to calm herself down as she continued unabashed. 'Kate, a move like this takes time, commitment and money — a lot of money, which we just don't have. You can't just up-sticks and go!' Hailey was really trying to quell the mixture of anger and anxiety.

'I'm a big girl now. You know, not nine! And I am serious. It's time I got out of this hole and made a life for myself, a real life, Hailey.' Kate sat down on the old sofa by the small electric radiator. 'Besides, Hailey, what would you know about London or anywhere? You wouldn't have moved away. You chose to stay here, you're a home maker. For one thing, it's nowhere near as cold down there as it is up here in the north. You've only ever lived up here. You never wanted to make the break and step out on your own. I do, so don't resent me for it. You know what they say, 'If you love them . . . let them go'.'

'And when was the last time you 'lived' anywhere else, Kate?' Hailey reminded her that her own knowledge of the world was somewhat lacking too.

'Yes, but that's about to change because I am taking control of my own life. You always wanted to go to university, so you go . . . I dare you.' Kate waved a finger at Hailey to stress her point and it was one that hurt her sister more than she knew. 'I'm going to London.' Kate opened her arms, making a sweeping gesture at the room. 'I've had enough of the 'Ebton Hilton'. Except for the odd youth hostelling trip around the Lake District or the wilds of Derbyshire, where else have we been?' Kate raised her eyebrows at her sister in defiance.

Hailey was more hurt by Kate's words than she cared to show. This 'hole' to her represented their lives. It was a council house, but it was where their mother had brought them up until her illness had become too severe for her to cope as the matriarchal figure, then most of the 'bringing up' had fallen onto Hailey's shoulders. It was a role she had grown into and had thought that Kate was always grateful for.

'This is our home.' Hailey stared at

Kate looking for some sign of acknowledgement for all the years she had stayed to look after her kid sister.

'Well, now it's all yours. I need to move out and on with my life. I love you, Hailey, but really I'm doing this for the both of us or we'll both die old maids together.' Kate pulled a ridiculous face, as if she were decrepit and old then crossed her arms and fell back onto the worn out cushions of the armchair.

When their father walked out to buy a bag of crisps and did not return over a decade ago, Hailey had struggled to help her mother through the shock, illness and lonely years. Her distraught eight year old sister looked to her for comfort and security, so Hailey had earned what little she could, doing part time jobs that fitted in with the demands that they both made on her time. Her life, her own dreams, had been suspended, but she cared for them both dearly, so dutifully she had stayed and been their rock. Even after her

7

mother's death it was Kate's well-being she thought of, and not her own. Hailey had promised her mum she would look after her sister, and it was a promise she had tried to keep. She had intended that Kate should have every chance to fulfil all the opportunities in life that fate had denied her. But watching the petulant, selfish face of her kid sister and her easy dismissal of the life they had shared, Hailey felt as though she had been swiped physically across the face, and it was a rebuttal that hurt her deeply.

'Have you really thought all of this through? If you have, why didn't you tell me about it before now?' Hailey's temper was high, but controlled now, quietly seething, it felt strange and dangerous to her. Those rare holidays in the Lake District and Derbyshire had been perfect in her eyes. They had laughed and played together, got soaked on long walks and then dried off in the sun. She had felt free, in a world that had so many restrictions upon her.

But only money could have freed her to do the things she desperately wanted to do. Hailey had a longing to return to her schooling by doing a degree in history or art, and travelling the world. But she had had to look after Kate and earn enough to make life bearable. Yet, now Kate was throwing her opportunity to go to university to the four winds in order to take a job in London, a city nearly three hundred miles away. Hailey's disappointment was outweighed only by a growing and overwhelming sense of fear. If Kate left her too, what would she do now? She'd only have herself to care for. She had been trapped in her role for so long that she had settled into the safety zone of her own rut.

'Listen, Hailey, I understand you like having me here, and I'm glad you feel that way. However, it's time for us to split up.' Kate put her arm around her big sister and squeezed her tightly. Hailey felt cold inside, numbed by the suddenness of the decision Kate had made, and without even discussing it with her. Perhaps she was right, Hailey began to wonder. Maybe she was being selfish and she should just let her go. But why was the decision being made so quickly? Two months ago they were discussing her options of going to university at either York or Durham. Hailey stopped panicking for a moment and subdued her emotions and started thinking; something was wrong. She was missing some vital piece of information, but what?

'Tell me more about this job you've applied for in the 'big' city?' Hailey pulled away and walked into the kitchenette to fetch her own cup of tea.

'I've already been accepted for it. I'm going to be Personal Assistant to Mr David Penwick.' Kate smiled warmly and Hailey instantly sensed there was more to this sudden change of direction in Kate's plans than disenchantment with her home or the sudden development of Kate using her common sense — hormones were involved!

'Who is Mr David Penwick, when he's at home?' Hailey asked, as she plonked herself down in her cosy armchair. She was a neat size twelve who spent her life in jeans, sweaters or baggy fleece tops and either boots or trainers. Her light brown shoulder length hair was as practical as she was. It hung heavy and straight but could easily be tied back when she needed it out of the way. If Hailey had ever thought about it, she was naturally attractive in a girl-next-door sense of the word. She was not a glamour model, nor a stunning beauty, but her fresh face and the inner warmth of her character shone brightly out of her deep blue eyes. But all Hailey saw was the plain image who had always stared back at her from the bedroom mirror. Kate, in contrast, had long legs, a slim body and had the soft hazel brown eyes of her father. She also had an inner confidence that Hailey had nurtured but had lacked herself.

'David's the Marketing Director of

'FITTS'.' Kate laughed as Hailey raised a quizzical eyebrow. 'OK, I'll save you the pain of guessing — it stands for 'First Information and Technology Training School', and when he is at home he is in a five bedroom, two reception, three bathroom house over in North Dalton — with its own indoor swimming pool and Jacuzzi!' Kate sipped her tea slowly, looking rather smug as she disclosed this new information to Hailey.

'David? Not Mr Penwick?' Hailey asked and noted Kate's face flushed slightly. 'You sound very knowledgeable about your new boss, Kate — and his home.'

'He doesn't stand on ceremony. He's a great guy,' Kate answered defensively. 'You'd love him, honestly.'

'You sound like you're very familiar with him. Is he tall, dark and handsome or short, fat and balding?' Hailey watched Kate carefully as her pink face deepened in colour slightly. Hailey realised instantly that the silly girl had got a thing for this bloke. She adopted her more motherly tone. 'How long have you known him, Kate?'

'About six months. He was running one of our modules and put the IT in place at the college. We hit it off straight away. He said I had great potential.' Kate stopped to sip more of her tea.

Hailey gulped down a mouthful, not really wanting to know anymore yet feeling that she had to look out for her headstrong sister. 'I've always told you that you have that, haven't I? If you work hard at university, life is an open door, or whatever cliché you want to describe it — Freedom! Believe me, it's not something you should toss aside so easily.' She stared at her sister, praying the girl would open her eyes and see the sense in her words.

'Yes, I know you've always said I have a great future ahead of me, but you would say that. You're my sister! David's different; he sees me as a person in my own right.'

Hailey looked straight at Kate really

trying hard not to lose her temper. 'What the hell do you think I see you as — a Martian?'

'No. Oh, I don't know — an extension of you — a child, your child or a replacement for Mum. Someone to look after and smother. What I mean is you always say that I can and will succeed, because you always do. But David only knows me as an adult, and he's been very impressed with what he's seen so far.'

Hailey was only just managing to prevent herself launching a tirade at Kate. A replacement for her mum, indeed! Why didn't she just say it — 'Get a life, Hailey,' instead of spelling it out. The ungrateful brat! 'So what has he seen of you so far?' Hailey asked pointedly, but Kate ignored her.

'Well, he's been so impressed that he's offered me the job.' Kate crossed her long legs, folding her hands over her knees.

'Wait a minute. If he has this mansion up here and is so impressed with your maturity and ability, why are you going to be working in London and where are you going to be living?' Hailey smelled a rat. A big, huge one, called David.

'He's leaving the family home and . . .'

'What family?' Hailey asked straight away. 'Does he live with Mummy?'

'No, his wife — she's a real cow. Always been playing around, led him a right dance. She will soon be his ex.' Kate managed to pour utter contempt into her voice. Then she smiled and, with radiant childish enthusiasm, continued, 'He has an office in London and a partner down there.'

'Male or female?' Hailey asked.

'Male! Don't be bitchy, Hailey, it does not become you. Anyway, David is selling up the home and the northern office and splitting the money with his ex. That way he'll make a clean break of it, before the big money rolls in, by concentrating all his efforts on the London office.' Kate looked even smugger.

'And for this he needs a PA? Why hasn't he already got one?' Hailey asked thinking what a naïve little fool her sister was.

'Well, he had but he's divorcing her — get it?' Kate's comments were really starting to upset Hailey, but she had coped with so many hard situations before that she was not about to let her sister, however foolish she was, know how much she was hurting inside.

'So you're the replacement! Get real, Kate, where will you be living? What duties are you replacing?' Hailey wished she'd cottoned on to David before they had got to this stage, but what could she do now? 'And when do you intend to move out of here?'

Kate fidgeted uneasily before standing up and answering her defiantly. Hailey knew her worst fears were correct when Kate did this because she had always used her height to try to force her opinion onto Hailey, as if being able to look down on her gave her some kind of superiority.

16

'I'm going to live in his flat until things are sorted out all around and we thought it would be best if we moved everything out of here a week on Monday.'

Hailey was glad she hadn't stood up for she was sure she would have collapsed back into the chair on hearing the deadline for the planned move.

'Do I get to meet this man before he whisks you off to his castle or are you just going to pack up and sod off without so much as a goodbye or a thank you?' Hailey was far from sure that she even wanted to meet him, for now she would always despise him for causing yet another huge rift in her life. This time with her only close family member and, yes, she had brought her up almost as if she were her own child. She had images of herself launching at this stranger like a wild cat, which was totally unlike her normal sane behaviour, but this 'David' had obviously swept her lovely, impressionable and intelligent sister off her feet. If only

Kate had inherited some of their mother's common sense, Hailey thought, then she would see just what a huge mistake she was about to make. Mind, she thought ironically, she herself had been blessed with buckets of the stuff and look where it had got her — nearly thirty, living in a 'hole' with her younger, ungrateful, sister. Single, with no prospects and now being thrown into a completely unnerving and unsure future. Hailey knew arguing would only embitter Kate and make her more determined to have her own way, but the temptation to do just that was great — or alternatively, equally attractive was the temptation to pack her bag for her this very night. Inconsiderate and selfish as Kate was, Hailey sighed with resolve, she would have to be strong again and deal with this like she dealt with every other crisis life had chucked her way. If her worst fears were realised, the best thing she could do would be to be there to pick up the pieces, if all else went wrong. A tempting thought crossed her mind, of deserting the ship herself and leaving Kate to sort out her own mess for a change. Blast it! Hailey was blessed with a conscience. She knew she'd do the right thing — she always did.

'Yes, you can meet David, tomorrow.' Hailey asked and looked around at their tidy but well worn home. 'Well loved' was what their mum had called it, but obviously it was an opinion not shared by Kate, Hailey thought.

'Not here, Hailey. He's taking us out to the Eastern Star.'

Hailey didn't like Kate's dismissal of their home as if it wasn't good enough for this 'David'. The name was already sticking in her throat.

'An Indian restaurant?' Hailey asked, hoping not. Curries were not usually on her menu.

'No, Chinese.' Kate rolled her eyes upwards as if Hailey knew nothing.

Perhaps, Hailey thought, perhaps she should have been firmer with her when she was a child instead of patiently talking her through her every trauma.

'So now, my dear big Sis, you and I

are going on a shopping spree.' Kate picked up her bag.

'With what?' Hailey asked. She had just been told her world was to be torn apart by the 'David thing' and Kate was talking about going shopping. 'With what?' Hailey repeated.

'Leave everything to me.' She reached into her bag and pulled out her purse. It seemed to have an unusually healthy number of notes trying to escape from it. 'With this!' She held up her purse. 'You are going to have a make over.' Kate beamed at her.

Hailey walked into the kitchenette and washed her cup in the plastic bowl.

'Where did that come from, Kate?' Hailey looked straight at her and she didn't like what she saw and heard.

'David, of course.'

'Why would he be giving his 'P.A. to be' such a large amount of cash?'

To Hailey's amazement Kate laughed at her.

'Hailey, I love you to bits, but before the next century moves onwards, will you please join the world in this one? David is a lovely guy. Over the last few months we have become like — you know, close. Yes, and before you ask, I do take care and I'm not a naïve little fool. I have no appropriate clothes to be a PA in, so he has given me some money to get decently kitted out, OK?'

'Then go ahead and enjoy yourself. That money has nothing to do with me. I have not earned it and I don't want any part of it. I'll find something to wear that will not embarrass you too much I hope.' Hailey slammed her mug onto the draining board.

Hailey turned back to the sink and started to wash it down. She wasn't terribly house-proud but as she scrubbed it she was having mental images of her hands grasping David's neck. It was very unnerving to her and not what she knew she should be feeling towards another member of the human race.

'Hailey, when will you ever look up and wise up? Or do you want to spend your whole life at the kitchen sink?'

Hailey was so angry she dared not speak to her. She gripped the cloth in her hand tightly.

'Don't put your Christian ethics onto me, Hailey. David and I love each other and, as soon as the divorce is through, we shall be married.'

Hailey put down her cloth silently. A cold rage was threatening to explode from her as she struggled to keep her control. Kate stepped back. She knew she had crossed Hailey's line and for the first time looked at her as if she had realised how much of an upset and a shock this whole business was to her older sister.

'I wish you and your 'lover' every happiness in your future lives. I have always wanted the best for you and for you to have every opportunity that has passed by me, but I have never **ever** preached my beliefs at you. You stopped going to Sunday school when you chose to and I never questioned it. I pray you will return but I have never tried to badger you into it or insist you do . . . '

'I know, I know, perhaps that was unfair, you just got me on the defensive . . . ' Kate interrupted.

'So please don't use that line on me again, Kate. You live by your beliefs and I'll live by mine. I don't want to have someone who is a total stranger to me buy me an outfit. OK? If I'm not good enough for you as I am, then tough!' Hailey walked out of the kitchen.

'I'm sorry, Hailey. I only meant to take you out for a treat. That was all. I didn't mean to get you so upset.' Kate smiled at her sheepishly.

'Well you did. Congratulations on your success . . . '

'And celebrations?' Kate shook her purse in the air.

'But I won't hold it against you if you cook my dinner tonight,' Hailey added as she dried her hands, trying to lose some of her anger.

'OK, why? What will you be doing?' Kate asked, as she put her purse back into her bag.

'Going out. I'll be back by half six.'

Hailey smiled back at her.

'May I ask where?'

'Yes, you may,' Hailey answered, but grabbed her coat and bag and headed for the door. She had to get out of her home, the only one she had ever known, to somewhere she could think in peace.

2

James Hood stood silently watching his plane depart from the airport terminal window. He'd missed it by minutes and had been offered a free drink in the first class lounge to appease him, and a transfer to another flight the next morning. This was supposed to be the start of a relaxing holiday. One crash on the M25 and he had been stranded without any means of moving either forwards or backwards. If he could have bought his way out of his dilemma he would have, but money couldn't move the cars that had clogged up the road ahead of him.

'Damnation!' he said out loud. His normally cool demeanour had been seriously rocked. Recently, even he had noticed just how crotchety he had become. Life used to be full of fun. Everything he had once seen as a challenge; the climb to success had been demanding but lucrative and satisfying until now. Recently something had changed within him. He was starting to suspect that 'the something' was his drive. His career had gained momentum, the stakes were higher now, as were the rewards, which had tightened their grip on him. It seemed the more successful he was the less time he had to enjoy it and the more he had to lose.

He'd needed to be on that flight. If he left on the next one he'd lose a whole day of his holiday — and he desperately wanted to get away. The sight of the ambulances on the motorway amidst the scattered wreckage had gnawed at his conscience as he cursed the delay it had caused him. That had been a surprise to him, because James didn't think he had any conscience left. He was exhausted; he rubbed his tired eyes with his hands, and sighed. Even this break had been planned so that he could still enjoy some luxury but return quickly if one of his account clients needed him urgently. Blake, his senior partner, drained him mentally with the constant targets he set. Meet one, and he'd produce an even tougher one for the next, always squeezing more out of each new account. He felt exhausted.

Then there was Michelle. He smiled as he remembered their last date. She was beautiful, fanciful, physically demanding and self centred. He leaned his tall frame against the large window. She was everything a man could wish for on the outside, but her persistent empty, vain banter was driving away what was left of his sane mind. Of course at first he was so pleased, couldn't believe his luck. Every guy in the office was jealous, including Blake, but, James had begun to realise there had to be more to life than this. He laughed to himself because he was well aware that many a man would consider even murder to have his current lifestyle. He stared at the runway, the next flight would be out soon.

'Excuse me, sir?' The gentle voice interrupted his thoughts and startled him.

'Yes, what is it?' He was tired and his voice was sharper than he had meant it to be. Turning around he saw a nervous old lady standing by his side. She looked as if she would fall over if he raised his voice any louder. Something deep down stirred inside him — a distant memory, because she reminded him of his grandmother. A faint recall of an uncomplicated childhood brought a smile to his face. 'Sorry,' he said, smiling reassuringly at her, trying to put her at ease in case he had behaved like an ogre. 'I was a little distracted. I missed my plane. I didn't mean to be so abrupt.' He shrugged his shoulders apologetically as if trying to excuse himself. Now it was he who was behaving nervously.

'Yes, I know you did. You see, I saw you arguing with the young lady at the check in,' the old lady said sheepishly.

James felt himself colour a little. They'd stopped him boarding because he had missed the closing time by ten lousy minutes. And the fact that he was a first class ticket holder had not made a slightest bit of difference because they were boarded already, and overbooked!

'I wondered . . . if you could . . . ' she was anxious, 'I wondered if you would help me. I have a serious problem, you see.'

James thought that perhaps she had a heavy bag or something that she may need lifting but she only had a handbag with her, which she clung to, along with an old shopping bag.

'Why, yes if I can. What can I do for you?' James asked her kindly. His dark brown hair was ruffled from the constant combing with his fingers as the frustration had mounted whilst he was stuck in that interminable road jam.

'You're booked on tomorrow morning's flight, aren't you?' Her eyes looked moist and her voice was unsteady.

'Yes, I am. They couldn't or wouldn't put me on the flight for today. Now I'm going to lose a whole day here in this dump. They wouldn't even put me late onto the first class compartment. I mean, what do we pay the extra for?'

The old lady's lip seemed to be quivering slightly.

'I'm sorry. I didn't mean to lose my temper again. It's just the frustration of it all.' He apologised again, amazed that he had done so twice in such a short time when it was a habit he had long since escaped from. His attention was taken by a young woman running across the lounge towards them.

'Gran! I've been looking all over for you.' The woman came over to where they were standing. 'Sorry, I hope she hasn't been pestering you. You must excuse her. We'll find some other way around the problem . . . somehow.' The young woman's face was very flushed.

'You don't get things, dear, if you don't ask,' the old lady said. 'All the economy seats have gone and nobody would let me have theirs. I saw this kind looking young man and thought I'd ask him — just in case he would let me have his ticket. I'll miss the wedding if I don't get on that plane tomorrow, Emma.' She looked desperately at James, her eyes watering as she spoke.

'You wanted my ticket?' James asked in disbelief. He spent his life knowing a good deal when he saw it. The old lady was 'desperate'. She'd pay anything, if she could, but first class would be beyond her, he was sure of that.

The old lady nodded back at him, hope springing from her eyes.

'Gran, you can't ask that!' The woman snapped at her then turned to James. 'I'm sorry. We got stuck in this awful snarl up on the motorway and she's very upset. The accident was a shock in itself without all of the disappointment at missing the plane. Please excuse her.' She steered the old lady gently away, but not before those sad grey eyes had locked onto James's one last time. 'Gran, you can't keep pestering people like this. People don't give up their holiday tickets like that unless you can pay double, and we can barely afford the economy class, first is out of the question.'

'Well, Mr Hodgkin gave up his seat to Mrs Jarvis on the Dorset coach so that she could see her daughter when she was having young Abigail,' the old lady said defiantly.

'That was a church trip. This is a major airport, Gran. You can't expect strangers to be so generous; it just doesn't happen that way. Times have changed.'

'Well not for the better then!' the old lady exclaimed.

'Wait!' James watched them as the old lady's face turned towards him. Her eyes shone with something he hadn't seen for quite some time — hope, not greed. 'Whose wedding is it?' he asked, as if it was any business of his anyway.

'My son, Eddie's. He sent us the tickets. My daughter has a seat on the plane, but I haven't. I can't travel on my own, you see. So she'll have to take me back home and come back here in time to catch the next one, by herself.'

'I doubt that will be possible. The roads won't be clear for some time. Here,' James looked at the face of hope and smiled broadly at her, 'take mine. My name is Mr Hood, James Hood, so we are no longer strangers.' He opened his briefcase, pulled out his ticket and handed it to her. 'We'll sort it out with the girls at the check in. They can change the paperwork and you can give me the money for the economy ticket and I'll bridge the gap between the two.' James could hardly believe what he was saying or doing but in an unusual way it felt quite good. He was making the old lady happy.

'But she can't pay. We haven't that kind of money!' the young woman said excitedly as she was obviously torn between disappointing her grandmother again and how she would cope with a large bill.

'Call it an early Christmas present,'

James quipped, and imagined that Blake would think he had completely lost his mind if he found out.

James arranged for the ticket transfer and for the old lady to get a little extra care on the flight. The two women were so moved he had both of them holding back tears of joy.

'We can't thank you enough,' the young woman said, and the old lady beamed broadly at him.

'Thank you. I knew you were a real gentleman. So few left today, you know.'

James grinned back at her. She was so like his grandmother — unassuming yet had a way with her that somehow coerced people into doing her bidding.

'You're a good person, Mr Hood,' she said, and touched his arm.

'No, that I'm definitely not. You just caught me in a moment of weakness.' He picked up his briefcase and turned to leave, but the old lady tugged the sleeve of his jacket. Her eyes seemed to open wide and peer straight into his deep brown tired ones.

'No, you are a good person, and what you did tonight required great strength not weakness. My thanks to you and God bless you. Be happy in your life,' she released his arm, 'You're like your namesake.'

'Gran!'

'James?' He looked at her laughing eyes as her daughter hugged her.

'No, Robin, of course.'

James laughed as he left them not knowing what to say. Something about the old lady touched him deeply and her words had penetrated. Yes, he was like Robin Hood, only he stole from the rich, but this was the first time he had given anything back to anyone, poor or not. He felt strange inside, humble almost — a very unusual feeling. The anger that had filled him had diminished and he was smiling again, at least for a few moments. Blake would have said he had been weak, soft even, and that his actions had been the height of stupidity. But in a strange way it really felt good; netting that two million pound account last week somehow hadn't been half as rewarding. This feeling came with no strings attached, whereas clinching a deal was only the first base on a long journey of contractual fulfilment and deadlines.

James thought he must be more tired than he realised and decided a good night's sleep in a decent hotel would set him right. He just hoped that when he awoke in the morning he wouldn't be too angry with himself for being such a soft touch. Now he had no flight to catch, no holiday planned. But, one thing he knew for sure, he had to get away.

3

Kate heard the phone ring at the other end of the line. She studied her nails looking for any blemishes in her polish as she waited for David to pick up the receiver. He must be there. She needed to talk to him, to hear his voice and have his reassurance.

'Hi, Kate.' The deep relaxed voice instantly brought a smile to her face. He had one of those clever phones that, like all the gadgets in his home, intrigued Kate. It told him who was calling so long as the number was stored in its databank. David lived in the 'here and now' and looked to the future. Her eyes glanced around their old house with all its oddments of furniture, eighties' or nineties' fashion mainly. She closed her eyes and visualised his home — it was like a small mansion to her and soon they would have their own place — in London! The future was filled with promise and he had promised her a lot.

'Hi, are you missing me?' she asked coyly.

'As ever. Are you coming over here tonight?' His voice betrayed his anticipation. She knew how to please him, and she smiled broadly because he did the same for her.

He was so sensitive, knowing just what to say and do. 'What about your wife?' Kate asked. They rarely spoke about Sonia. Well, David did, but always in derisive tones. It was his way of showing her that he had no love for the woman and to make Kate feel special.

'She has gone to stay with her mother for the weekend. She's saying it's too upsetting for her to be around me, in her 'condition'.' He laughed, but it was an empty hard laugh, full of loathing and contempt.

'What condition is that?' Kate's voice rose slightly. There was only one thing that Kate could think of that he was hinting at. If Sonia was pregnant, it could change everything. David might become broody and he could decide to stay with her. If he changed his mind now, how would she ever smooth Hailey down again? He had even spoken to her saying how he wanted to have a son . . . one day, before he was forty. That was ages away yet, at least five years. So Kate knew they had heaps of time together for fun, during which she would turn his opinion around. He'd discover what it was to be young and free with her. Once they were in the city, living the high life, there would be no time for his daydreams of his own dynasty; the reality of nappies did not blend well with the image he had drawn for her. Kate had no wish to become a mother hen.

'She says she's up the spout, damn her,' David sighed. 'She's lying of course; it's just a last ditch attempt to keep me — out of desperation.'

'But how could she be? I mean, it can't be yours. How far gone is she?'

Kate's mind was reeling. She and David had been sleeping together regularly for four months. He'd said that he and his wife were no longer on intimate terms. Her stomach felt a huge knot forming in it. Had her David being lying to her?

'Three or four months she reckons.' David sighed heavily again. 'It's not for real, Kate. Don't let her get to you.'

'But that's impossible — I mean, you know that it definitely can't be yours — if it exists at all. Can it?' Kate tried to sound calm and reasonable but the emotions she was feeling were starting to filter through to her voice. She felt threatened, jealous and uncertain of what to say and do. Sonia seemed to be holding all the trump cards. She thought about the money in her purse and decided she would fight every inch of the way. David loved her, they were good together and their future was going to be bright. She would not let Sonia mar it.

'Look, 'if' it is mine — that's if the cheating cow is telling the truth, which

I sincerely doubt — it will have been my parting visit to her when we had that big launch party here. Do you remember, we were just getting to know one another then and, well . . . I was a bit four sheets to the wind by the end of it? Don't panic. It's not going to change a thing. I'll insist she have a DNA test or whatever they do and, 'if' it's mine, I'll throw the BMW into the settlement too. It's what she's bloody wanting anyhow — my blood and more money. In the meantime, I've got a private eye trying to fix her up, you know, so there is reasonable doubt as to the parentage due to her affairs. So how're things with you? Have you told big Sis, yet?'

'Oh yes, and it went very well — Not!' Kate's voice dropped to a quiet subdued whisper. 'She didn't take it too well. Perhaps I should have said something to her before now. I think it was quite a shock, you know; she's used to having me around. I think we should have been more open about our plans. She thought I would be going to university in York or Durham. We had been working towards that for years.' Kate felt a surge of guilt as she saw for the first time how much of a blow it must have been to Hailey.

'Absolutely not! I've told you before, stick with me and I'll teach you everything you'll ever need to know.' He chuckled to himself. 'On everything!'

'You're wicked.' Kate laughed. David's voice sounded so strong and masterful to Kate. She had never had a patriarchal figure in her life, and David made her feel as though he would protect and guide her always. She'd never want for anything ever again. She smiled and hugged herself as she listened to his words.

'Look, she's cosseted you your whole life, you were so naïve . . .' His voice trailed off with what Kate thought was a patronising note.

'Well, I'm not anymore, am I?' Kate responded sharply. She didn't mean to but it had been a tender subject to her for so long. Nearly all her friends had slept with boys, one well before sixteen, or at least they had boasted that they had.

'Kate love, I didn't mean it badly against you. Hey, I told you you're my precious gemstone, a prize jewel and I'll never let you go. Unlike that lying bag I married. She'd had more partners than a co-operative. I just meant it was time that you lived your own life now. Besides, just because she's happy being the single ice-queen doesn't mean that you have to follow suit. Anyway, you'd be doing her a big favour.' He chortled again.

'David! She isn't. I'm sure she's had her own flings; she is such a loving person,' Kate replied indignantly.

'Want to bet?' David laughed.

'I've never asked her, David, and I'm not about to start now.' Kate couldn't help but laugh, too, embarrassed at the thought, yet for the first time she was curious to know. 'It would be like asking your mum. She's not a kid sister, you know.'

'Yeh, I know. Perhaps she's a man hater. Didn't you say your dad took a hike and left her to look after you and your mum? Stands to reason then, she might have a ball of resentment deep within her.'

'I know what you mean and she's not, I'd know. She's OK, David, honest. Perhaps once I'm out of her hair she'll find someone — after all she's not that old.' Kate thought for a moment. The idea of Hailey finding a partner had never occurred to her before now. She presumed she hadn't been bothered, but perhaps it was that the opportunity hadn't presented itself because of her sense of duty to the family.

'How old?' David asked.

'Nearly thirty,' Kate answered, thinking actually that was quite old and wondering if her sister had ever slept with anyone at all. She couldn't imagine it.

No, Hailey was just too boringly good — a rare and threatened species. Perhaps, Kate thought, she should put an endangered species sign on her door.

'Well maybe you could let me charm her and I'll soon find out and put her right. Her clock's ticking past its sell-by date.' David laughed but Kate didn't. She felt a surge of mixed loyalties combined with . . . jealousy. 'Only joking, kid,' he added. 'I'm sure I'll love her on sight as my own little sis. Look, I've got to go. You coming over tonight or not?'

'Not!' She knew how much he wanted her. David did not answer. 'Got you! Pick me up at nine.' Kate heard a sigh of relief escape his lips.

'OK, you little tease. I'll be there. You be ready, I've got something special for you . . . ' His voice trailed off waiting for her anxious response. She did not disappoint him.

'What, tell me, please?'

Now it was his turn to tease. 'See you, Kate, at nine.'

The phone line burred as he hung up at the other end. Kate wondered where Hailey had gone to in such a foul mood. It would be strange without her around daily. Whatever Hailey's faults, she had always been the one person Kate could completely rely on. She replaced the phone receiver and smiled to herself, knowing that now she had her David, and her life had only just begun for real.

★   ★   ★

Hailey walked up to the large wooden door in the side of the old sandstone church. She turned the iron-ringed handle but the door did not open. God's house was closed to her. She took a few steps back and stared up at the turreted tower; it was a sad reflection of the times, she thought, that the doors had to be kept locked when the church was unattended. So much for being my sanctuary, Hailey muttered to herself.

She felt the breeze on her face and followed its scent. The salty air led her to her favourite place, the flat sandy beach of her childhood. Crossing the High Street, Hailey disappeared down the only remaining old alley of the redeveloped town. 'Old Jerusalem' it was known as. It was dark and narrowed near a sharp bend. It reminded her of the days when, as a child, she'd dare herself to run down it to take the short cut to her nana's house. She smiled fondly at the memory. That was before her mother became ill, when their family was a happy one, when she was allowed to be young, when she had two parents to take responsibility for all the serious things in life and she could play with her baby sister.

She passed the Italian ice cream parlour; again memories flooded her mind of knickerbocker glories and laughter. She crossed the coast road. The Yorkshire cobles, the traditional flat-bottomed fishing boats, still lined the broad promenade. She took a deep breath and looked out across the bay. From the headland to the south, and the river mouth to the north, the huge sweeping coastline featured dunes, marshes and miles of fine sand. Hailey climbed over the sea wall and ran down the banked slope. She shoved her hands deep into her coat pockets as the cold air chilled her through to her bones.

The sea's roar became ever louder as incoming waves crashed against retreating waves. The white horses rose and sank as the water's spray dispersed back into its own mass. Hailey watched in awe at the mighty force, yet, as she approached the shoreline, each ripple on the sand ran quietly out of energy and slipped back. Hailey bent down and picked up a skimming stone. She threw it hard knowing it would not skip across the water's surface, but sink beneath the waves. That was how she felt, like she was sinking, yet knowing deep within her that she would rise and float again. It was the pattern of her life. It was just at the moment she did not feel as though she had the energy to fight her way back up and start all over again.

Everything she had worked for her whole life, her family, Kate's future, had suddenly slipped away from her and she felt as though she was going to be left to sink. What on earth was she to do with herself? She'd never been on her own before. All the things she had wanted to do, but had not been able to because she had had Kate to consider, could now happen. But without warning, discussion or consideration, her sister had been planning this and never said so much as one word to her. Why? When had she ever turned Kate away? The answer was simple, never. She had always listened to her and helped her. Hailey shook her head in dismay. How could she abandon all they had together so easily? Tomorrow she had to face the unseen enemy — the 'David'.

Yet, despite her feelings of rejection and devastation, Hailey knew she would meet him, with good grace and a smile. Why? She'd do it for Kate, of course; like she always had. If it was too late to stop her then she would let her go with good grace and try to be there for her if all went wrong. But by then, Hailey realised she might have her own agenda established and Kate would have to accept that and adapt. Or, it may be the best thing for the both of them. The answer lay in the future and Hailey knew from experience the only way to deal with that was to welcome it and handle it one day at a time.

★ ★ ★

James woke up thinking about a golden beach, imagining a warm pool and a relaxing drink in his hand as he lay back on the lounger. Instead, he stared out of the hotel window across a car-congested street. Standard hotel furnishings surrounded him, a small plastic kettle and a tiny cup. He emptied the sachet of coffee into it and filled the kettle with water. He pulled on his clothes and poured the tiny amount of milk into the cup — it curdled as soon as it met the boiling water. The rain tippled down outside streaking the hotel window. They needed a good wash anyway, as the streaks cut through the murk.

James laughed at Murphy's Law, which he seemed to have fallen under and threw the plastic into the bin. He thought about the old lady, Mrs Elliot, and wondered how she was enjoying her first class journey. His life, he felt was the pits. Nothing went right for him anymore. He checked out and walked over to the M6 and climbed in. He sat there. Where am I going? he asked himself and had no idea. He could hang around the airport, or get on any flight to almost anywhere, but what was the point? He wanted to get away from people, to have some space of his own — to think. So he drove south, and found himself wanting to see the sea again; any sea as long as he could stare at the open expanse of water. The gentle roaming hills of the downs gave way to the coastal ports. Somewhere deep in his childhood memories he remembered going to Southampton and seeing the ferries. He had wanted to go on one, but those days his parents could not afford to take him. He didn't have that problem now. He'd planned to spend five grand on this week's holiday so he still had plenty on his budget. He chuckled; he even set targets for his own holidays. He saw a huge ship at harbour. Now that's something, he thought, but then saw the name, 'The Queen Mary 2', and sighed. Shame, he thought, it would have made a change but he'd never make it back in time, so he kept following the road signs for the docks. A few traffic lights and speed traps later, he saw the Isle of Wight ferry terminal and decided, as he had never been there, why not? He only needed time to think and cut himself off. Who would find him there? So James boarded a ferry and, before he even realised what precisely he was doing, he was heading down the Solent, on his way to the Island.

Leaving his precious car crammed in

next to all manner of vehicles in the bowels of the ferry, he ventured up the narrow and steep stairwell, past the lower decks and stood on the bow of the upper deck as it smoothly moved away.

The water was a mass of activity. Catamarans, ferries, yachts, fishing boats, speedboats and cargo ships all vied for space.

The breeze was crisp, bracing and cool. His hair was blown by the wind but it was strangely exhilarating. He watched the mainland fade and was amazed to think he had travelled to the Far East and back, yet had never crossed the narrow stretch of water to this small island. Why he was doing it he had no idea, but it felt right, so he was content just to drift along for a change.

He saw a couple, hugging each other warmly. Part of him yearned for that sort of love — not hungry, greedy and always wanting something more, like Michelle, but cosy, close and content.

He wondered if he'd ever find such a woman.

'I think that's where the Queen Elizabeth docks, that is. I saw the Queen Mary back there, did you?' The young voice interrupted his blissful nothingness — his precious space, but he remembered the way he'd snapped at the old lady, so decided to smile as he looked down. His face froze as he saw the child.

'Sorry, mister, were you wanting to be left in peace?' the young lad asked.

'No, no, I didn't realise anyone was there, that's all.' James stared as if a magnetic force pulled his eyes downwards, trying not to, but feeling at a loss as to what to say again, for the youngster was in a wheelchair. This auburn haired child was chatting away to him as if he had not a care in the world.

'Billie's me name,' the lad cheerfully informed him.

'I'm James. Where's your mum and dad, Billie?' James looked around but there did not seem to be anyone looking after him.

'Well, Miss Reynolds has just popped to the toilet, but she'll be back soon. I don't have a mum and dad as such, but I live in Green Gables, near Puckpool beach. It's great. Do you know it?' The child's enthusiasm was infectious but James wondered how he could get any joy from a beach in his situation.

'Sorry, Billie, there was a queue.' A middle-aged woman bounced up to them; she was equally large in frame and character. 'Has this gentleman been keeping you busy whilst I was away?' The woman talked to the child but James was aware that her eyes were sizing him up.

James thought of the contrast between the old lady whose daughter apologised for her and this lady who made no apology for the lad at all. James realised she was right; there was no need to.

'No, Billie has been keeping me busy. Actually, I was just thinking that it's a bit cold out here. Would you like to have a drink in the warmth of the lounge?' He watched the child's face light up. James's world appeared to be changing daily. Normally he'd be wining and dining executives, selling the promotional packages that his team had worked so hard on, trying to keep his temper as clients nit-picked just to bring down the price or assert their own opinion. Yet, here he was thinking of offering two complete strangers a drink — a disabled child and his wholesome minder. He thought of the old lady at the airport and decided it was definitely a change. He just hoped it would satisfy his much needed rest.

'Would I? Then you can tell me about your fancy car. I saw you drive on the ferry. It's cool — a BMW, isn't it?' Billie started wheeling his chair towards the lounge doors.

'Convertible,' James said, and winked at the boy.

'This is really kind of you,' Miss Reynolds said as they followed behind.

'Not really. If anything, it's selfish. I

was feeling the chill and thought we'd all be more comfortable inside the sheltered area. Tell me, is he usually that cheerful?' James asked.

'No, he's human like all of us, but he has learned to be determined and thankful for all that he can do. I just wish we could offer him more, because his world is about to change and not for the better I'm afraid.' The woman looked down as she spoke to him. She seemed to force a smile back onto her face, as she looked up again. James realised she was trying to keep something from the boy.

'You live in a place called Green Gables at Puckpool I am informed.'

'You are informed correctly, at least for now, because we may not be able to stay there much longer.' Her words were said honestly, but James felt the pain hidden in them deeply, which surprised him, and over the course of the next half an hour, James's perspective on life would change forever. He listened intently as Miss Reynolds explained how her ideal home, Green Gables, was actually under threat.'

'How can you be so happy if the place you have worked so long for is going to be reclaimed?' James asked his new friend.

'Because, we believe that somehow it won't happen,' answered Miss Reynolds.

'But you said it was due to. Sorry, I don't understand.' James watched as the two people opposite him looked at each other and grinned warmly.

'We've asked for help,' Billie announced confidently.

'From the banks?' James asked, thinking their time had just been cut down, 'Ms Reynolds.'

'Please call me Sarah. No, we've visited all the churches where we know people and asked for prayerful support from the congregations. The banks are not being at all positive at the moment, so we have tried to find support elsewhere until we can resolve the problem.' Sarah looked straight at James who had to stifle the urge to laugh.

'Do you think God will send you the money you need?' James looked at Billie.

'We didn't ask for the money off God,' Billie said.

'No,' interrupted Sarah with undisguised enthusiasm, 'although it would be nice if it just turned up.'

'No, we asked them to pray that someone would be sent to us who knew how to help us, someone with a clear foresight, so that we can learn to help ourselves more.' Billie laughed at James's speechless face. 'We don't just want to sit waiting for handouts; we want to be able to support ourselves in some way.'

'What was it you said you did for a living, Mr Hood?' Sarah asked with a hopeful earnest expression on her face.

He looked at them and said, 'I give already wealthy people and firms the knowledge and profile they need to help them earn even more money. I work very long hours, get paid heaps more than I'm worth and am usually too tired or stressed to enjoy it.' He looked at their two faces as they smiled knowingly at each other. 'Believe me, I'm not the answer to anyone's prayers — more the cause of them needing support. I'm exceedingly selfish and like my creature comforts. Please call me James.'

'Do you enjoy what you do?' Billie asked.

'Yes and no. I used to. The challenge and adrenaline was a great buzz. I've a beautiful car, apartment and an almost ex girlfriend . . . '

'In that order?' Sarah asked.

'Precisely, my life is in the wrong order which is why I decided to take some time out and get right away from the city . . . '

'So you came to the Isle of Wight?' Billie asked and looked really confused.

'No, Billie, that was not my original intention. I was going to fly to . . . well, never mind. I wasn't supposed to be here and I can't imagine why I am telling you two all this. I do apologise. I must definitely need a break.' James suddenly felt very embarrassed.

'Don't apologise. You were meant to meet us, I'm sure. Where are you staying, James?' Sarah asked the question as if she already knew what his answer would be.

'Nowhere. I haven't booked in anywhere,' James admitted shyly.

'Stay with us then. Please?' Billie's voice was filled with an infectious optimism.

Sarah looked at him. 'The accommodation is warm, welcoming and basic, but you're more than welcome to stay, come and go as you please. Pay only for your food.'

'No wonder you need to raise money with an attitude like that. I'd be pleased to stay and pay my way, perhaps for a night or two. I could make a few suggestions that might help you and your plight. But I'm sure this meeting was purely a coincidence, nothing else. I don't like raising expectations unrealistically.' He stared at Sarah, who smiled back unabashed.

'We never raise our expectations unrealistically. We merely give thanks for all life's little 'coincidences'.'

The announcement over the loud-speaker told everyone that they were to return to their vehicles. James left them, and sat purposefully in his car, ready to follow the rusty blue people carrier to his temporary address, aware that he was no longer feeling lonely. In fact, he had found a sort of purpose, some new and very different friends and the space he had craved to take his mind of his own problems. But what on earth was he doing becoming involved in someone else's? The queue moved on and so did James, into a totally different world. 'Thank God for that,' he said and laughed at himself and the reference.

4

Hailey watched Kate waving frantically from the window of David's flash car as he drove her away. She smiled at her younger sister and saw tears stream down Kate's face. All Hailey could do was wave back as three words drifted around in her mind, 'Stupid little fool!'

The meetings between her and David had been pleasant enough, polite, although few, but Hailey was sure she had the measure of him. He wanted someone young and impressionable to manipulate into his ideal partner. His wife had had more sense and broken free. Kate's mind had been filled with tales of his wife's deceitful behaviour, but Hailey doubted if David's recount of events was accurate, as he spoke of her with such venom. Mind, he had a way about him that was pleasant enough and, physically, Hailey had to admit, he was tall, dark and very handsome. The trouble was, he was only too aware of it. He spent more time looking in the mirror and adjusting his attire than Kate did, and that was long enough — what a pair they made, Hailey thought to herself.

'She's gone then?' The familiar voice of their neighbour broke through Hailey's thoughts as the car vanished from her view. She was so annoyed with Kate that she felt strangely calm and had no compunction to shed a solitary tear. Strange, Hailey wondered why. Perhaps she was in denial or something, or was she just numb from the sudden change of events.

Simon stopped by her gate. His fair tousled hair was in stark contrast to David's, as were his grubby fleece and well-worn jeans.

'Yes, she's gone.' She looked at her friend. He must have been about the same age as David but was wiry and years of drinking and smoking at the club, where he played darts and snooker, had left a rather more rugged look to him; sort of more Robert Redford as opposed to Pierce Brosnan.

'How long do you give it then, Hailey?' Simon asked.

'Oh, he'll have her married within the year.' Hailey's answer was honest. 'That's if he can push his divorce through.' She had no doubt David had the prize he sought. He was not going to ditch Kate, but trap her in a gilded cage. The thing was, Kate just couldn't see it, and Hailey had not had the time to talk to her about it. Even if she had, it would sound like sour grapes. Hailey was in a 'no win' situation, David had seen to that.

'You reckon? Don't think he'll show her the city lights and move on then?' Simon was staring straight at Hailey's face. He'd been their neighbour for nearly ten years and had been a huge support to Hailey. Anything from fixing the fence to helping pick up their mother when she had fallen badly in the kitchen, all the while Simon had been there. He'd seen her father take a walk of no return. Just left them, the whole family, because he couldn't cope with their mum's illness, but Simon had helped now and then when he could. The thing was, though, if her dad couldn't cope, how had he expected them to? Did he even stop to consider that? It was all water under the bridge now and Hailey had decided long ago that her father was selfish and weak. It was a fact she had accepted but didn't dwell on, or at least she had tried not to. It was just that all this sudden change of events with Kate had brought so many memories back to her — some quite painful. At least Simon had stepped into the void and helped her to see her way through the stunned days that had followed, but sometimes friendship can come at a heavy price.

'No, Simon, I think he wants her for the long run. But will she want him when the novelty has worn off? Stupid, foolish, girl! If only she'd stopped and thought about how near she had been to going away to university with people of her own age. She has her whole life ahead of her and she's blown it on the first male to pay her any attention.' Hailey shook her head dismissively and cringed at the uncomfortable feelings of 'déjà vu'. At least Kate was deeply in love, or lust, and her world was going to broaden for better or worse. She was about to experience life in a way Hailey had only dreamed about. Well, actually being hitched to a control freak like David would be more of a nightmare to her.

Automatically Simon placed his arm around her shoulders. 'Come on, lass, have a cup of tea with Si. Forget about Kate and that David and think about yourself for a change.' He turned her around and walked her back into the house.

That was it; those simple words opened the floodgates. That was what she had to do, think of herself for a change — so simple, so tempting and so completely foreign to her.

For the first few moments Simon hugged her to him. Hailey felt the comfort of his arms around her and enjoyed the feeling of security they brought. She paused for a while to wonder if that was what Kate had craved, but dismissed it, because she knew that Kate enjoyed more than comfort in David's arms. He'd hooked her, body and soul.

Simon kissed her gently on her cheek. Instantly Hailey pulled herself together, separating from his embrace. She flushed red, quickly reaching for two mugs from the wooden tree that held them.

'I didn't mean to make you feel awkward, Hailey.' Simon folded his arms and leaned against the sink; so relaxed and at home in her kitchen.

'I know you didn't. Tea or coffee?' Hailey asked, and tried to force a smile. She was aware how she sounded — like someone of her mother's generation rather than a comparatively young, now free and single, woman.

'Tea,' he answered and stepped up behind her, placing his hands gently on her waist. Leaning forwards he kissed her neck softly, sensitively. She could smell the stale smoke on his jacket, and feel his moist lips against her skin. They made Hailey cringe.

'Don't, Simon, please stop this!' Hailey stepped away and switched on the kettle. He stared at her with a familiar look of longing in his eyes.

'Why not, Hailey? She's out of your hair now. You're free. We can do what we like, whenever . . . right now for instance.' He smiled but Hailey could only feel a heavy foreboding grip her, as she looked at him.

'You're not free, Simon,' Hailey snapped back, referring to his wife. She was trying to divert his attention and not respond to his suggestions.

'She doesn't count for anything and you know it. She had an affair. We're finished, have been for years. She's only interested in the kids and her soaps. You know she's only staying with me until

Emily does her exams, then she'll find her own place. Another five months, that's all and then we're both free, Hailey. Just think what we can do together. That bloke came just at the right time, eh?' Simon grinned and took a step towards her. 'We could move in here. It's better that way, this corner plot. It's bigger than mine, and the garden is in a better way. Then we could go abroad somewhere — Guernsey or Jersey, eh? You'll get a better job now you don't have to pay out to keep that little sis in college and so we can save to go wherever we want to. That new supermarket's taking on staff. If you hurry up you might get one of them till jobs. Then you'll get food tokens and stuff. Yep, the future is looking great, lass.' He sat down at the table and helped himself to a biscuit.

Hailey was stunned. Kate had hardly left the county and Simon was already mapping out her new living for her. He only needed the comfy slippers to put on his feet that were securely tucked under her table. Trapped — that's what she felt, here in her own home — not his home. She could work as a till girl to pay for their holidays. Absolutely, no way!

'Kate hasn't even left the town yet and you're talking like this! What on earth have you been thinking about these last few years? Simon, look I know you've been a really good neighbour to me. I appreciate your friendship but I need time to think about what I am going to do with my own life now. I don't want us to be anything more or less than the friends we are.' Hailey folded her arms in front of herself and stared defiantly back at him. 'Besides, I have a part time job and I've just sat my exams.'

'Exams! 'O' levels at your age,' Simon giggled, mocking her efforts to better herself.

'They're not called that now, and anyway I took them two years ago. I've been taking further exams in childcare.'

'Whatever, a test is a test and you

deserve more. We passed the 'just good friends' line a long while back. Don't tell me you've not hankered for me since then and waited for this day to come, like I have.' He was standing in front of her.

She shifted uneasily at the memory. How could she tell him that the 'experience' for her had not been that great, and how she had paid dearly for it. 'No, I'm definitely not going to tell you any such thing. That was something that should never have happened. I was so young and Mum had gone. It was a very vulnerable time for me and you should have seen that it was. Perhaps you did. It was something that should be left in the past. Please leave, Simon. Please?' Hailey sidestepped.

He bent forward and kissed her cheeks gently. 'All right I'll go. I've maybe rushed you a bit. But Hailey, you'll soon see this day as the best one of your whole life. As soon as Paula clears out, I'm all yours. Don't say it never should have happened. You was a bit young, granted, but you're a woman now and nothing can hold us back — not now, you're free.' He kissed her once more, with a desperation and hunger that scared Hailey. She could not help herself. She gasped in horror as she realised his delusion.

'Told you. You're waiting for me.' He slapped her bottom patronisingly and possessively, then left her shocked, in her own kitchen, looking at two mugs but knowing there would only be a need for one.

Hailey studied the mug in her hand. It was one she bought years before. The inscription on it read, 'Life's like a huge juicy sandwich. You only get out of it as much as you put into it!'

She threw it crashing across the kitchen floor and grabbed her coat. Hailey did not know if Simon heard the door slam, or whether he saw her storm off towards the seafront, but he didn't follow her and that was all she cared about. She walked through the edge of town, and followed the old panion way to the back of the churchyard. She breathed in the salt sea air, and made for her special place at the back of the grounds. There she crouched silently by the old oak tree, and prayed.

Later, walking along the beach, remembering the words of the well read poem 'Footsteps' she waited for an answer to come to her. It felt as though it was blocked whilst she was preoccupied by her past and the fear she felt of an unknown future ahead of her.

5

'James! James! Are you getting up?' Billie's voice echoed up the stairs of the old Victorian house.

'Billie, hush boy. You can't badger our guest like that. Honestly!' Sarah wheeled Billie back down the hallway and into the kitchen. The way had been cleared of all obstacles and a ramp enabled his chair down to access the levelled kitchen.

'Well it's 8.30a.m. It's not like he hasn't slept in.' Billie manoeuvred his chair up under the oak table.

Ten minutes later James walked in wearing a cable knit sweater and jeans. He looked pulled together, his hair roughly finger combed. 'Did someone call me?' he asked in an amiable manner amazed that he hadn't minded being woken from his sleep so abruptly, a sounder sleep than he had had for months. Must be the sea air, he thought.

'I'm so sorry, James. It was Billie, he's rather impatient at times. He thinks because he wakes up with the birds that everyone else should also. You go back to bed if you like; it's your holiday after all.' Sarah poured herself a coffee after setting Billie's breakfast tray in front of him. The boy looked at her with a heavy scowl.

'What and miss the chance of having company for breakfast?' He smiled at them both and Sarah poured him a much-needed coffee.

'So what are you doing today?' Billie asked and his eyes were full of undisguised hope.

'I thought I might take the car for a spin around the island,' James answered and watched the cloud come across Billie's face. 'Trouble is I've never been to deepest Wight before and have no one to show me where to go.' The cloud passed away again and James glanced at Sarah hoping he hadn't started something he shouldn't have.

'I'd show you the island. It would be great. Can I, Miss Reynolds?' Billie looked longingly at her.

'Well, I should say no. After all we're not that well acquainted.' Sarah looked at James.

'I've a clean record, except for being totally wrapped up in myself for the last ten years. I'd really appreciate it as it would get my grey cells working as to how to help you out here. You do need help, don't you?' James looked at Sarah who solemnly looked back and nodded.

'A year ago pride would have me say no, but we live and learn and their needs are greater than my personal pride. Yes, I . . . they desperately need help. You see, we had wanted to do up this place and have it as a sort of respite home for children like Billie. However, without George here to do the work I did not realise just how much the renovations would cost and I can't take in youngsters until the place has been finished and meets all health, safety and insurance demands. Billie's different because he's here to stay with me. He's George's son, but we can only stay here if I complete what we both started. Otherwise we will have to move elsewhere and, instead of making the place a home and a living, we shall no doubt just have to get by on our own. I'm adopting him, you see.'

'We?' James asked.

'Me and George, my hubby to be, bless him, but the good Lord took him last June and I'm not the one who was the builder by trade.' She shrugged her shoulders and said, 'Never mind, it's not our place to question. You enjoy your drive and come back inspired, please. I know you've a fast car, but please don't . . . I mean you'll take care, won't you . . . '

'I'll be good. I'll stick within the speed limit I promise. We'll come back safe and inspired. Take a notepad with you, Billie.' James winked at Sarah and repeated his promise to bring Billie back safe and sound.

'Sure,' Billie answered and wheeled

off down the hall.

'So how long have you got before you have to move from here, if you do nothing now?' James asked, sensing the feeling of impending doom that hovered over the place.

'Two, perhaps three months. You see I owe nearly a thousand pounds already.' She blushed, obviously embarrassed at what she considered her own inadequacy.

'When all is quiet tonight, let me see the accounts and your business plan . . . '

'Business plan?' Sarah looked at him obviously embarrassed. 'George had all of that in his head. We discussed and agreed things, but he was so good at organising his work, I didn't like to interfere. Only now, without him, I realise I should have known more.'

'I'll see what I can do to sort this mess out for you, but I'll make you no promises.' James smiled at her reassuringly. 'We shall come up with some ray of hope, I'm sure — two heads are better than one.'

'I shouldn't agree. I don't know you, it wouldn't be right, but we're desperate. We have made friends here but too many give different opinions and I think some people we know would like to buy the Gables now, whilst it still needs work.' Sarah looked at him.

'You prayed, didn't you? — I'm here, you have faith, and I'll try to dig deep and find some of my own.' James did not wait for a reply. He lifted his leather jacket off the chair and picked up Billie, carrying a very excited child to his car. As he placed the boy inside the passenger seat he suddenly realised it was the first time he had been able to share the real joy of his car with a fellow enthusiast, someone who wasn't masking jealousy, or enjoying it as a fashion accessory but showing honest appreciation. James knew he was going to really enjoy his holiday. He felt appreciated, and it was a new and pleasant feeling.

They drove by the coast road. The steep inclines of Ventnor provided little obstacle for them and the open stretch of road beyond Shanklin and Blackgang let them feel the sea breeze whilst admiring the beauty of the cliff views. James pulled into a viewpoint and stopped a while. 'It is lovely here.' Billie looked at him.

'I wish my dad was alive to meet you. He liked cars too.'

'Billie, why do you call Sarah Miss Reynolds, when she was to be your step-mum?' James thought he may have been stepping on sensitive ground but Billie laughed.

'Oh, I call her it when she bosses me around. She used to be my nurse. She did home care stuff when I was recovering from the accident. At first I didn't like the fact that Dad became fond of her, but then he went too.' The boy turned away from James. 'Hey, do you own a yacht?'

'No, I like to keep my feet on the ground most of the time, but I like looking at them, why?' James could see that Billie wanted to change the subject so followed the boy's lead.

'If you follow the road around you'll come to Yarmouth harbour. I know a place where we can get a drink and an ice cream if you want.'

James started the car. 'Lead on, I haven't had an ice cream for quite some time,' he admitted.

'Then it's time you had some fun,' said Billie as they headed for the open road.

★ ★ ★

'Hailey, I've got some brilliant news.' Hailey could not help but grin. This was the second piece of 'brilliant news' that Kate had had in as many days. The first piece had been the announcement of the forthcoming marriage. No big surprise there, Hailey had thought. She'd only been down south for two months. David had wasted no time at all. He had obviously paid his solicitors well to press on with the divorce. She wondered what he had promised his 'ex' to drop her resistance to it.

'You're already married?' Hailey said sarcastically.

'No, don't tease me. David's let me choose our house. It's lovely. It's in a tree-lined avenue. Four bedrooms, a study, a conservatory, three loos, an aga in the kitchen, fortunately there is a microwave too and the garden is landscaped and within walking distance of the sea.' Kate hardly stopped to breathe. 'You'll love it. I know you will'

'It sounds very nice.' Hailey didn't really know what to say. Kate seemed happy; perhaps she too needed a David. Simon was becoming more and more of a problem each day. Nothing she said dissuaded him about their different futures. 'However, it will not be me who will be living there, Kate.'

'You've just got to come down and see it, though.' Kate paused for a moment.

'I will be at the wedding, won't I?' Hailey asked. She presumed she was to be invited. 'You can give me a guided tour before the ceremony.' She was trying to avoid sarcasm with difficulty.

'You'll have to come down before that. Hailey . . . please? Tell me you will. There is so much to do. David said he'll pay for your ticket and have you collected at the station.' Kate was almost pleading with her, which Hailey could not help but feel annoyed at. After all, it was her decision to move, not Hailey's. Yet, she seemed as though she was being drawn into Kate's life as she always had been before. But wasn't that why Kate wanted to move away.

'I have things to do here. I've just enrolled on a work experience course and I'm trying to get a full-time job in the council crèche . . . ' Hailey added as she thought of the persistent sarcasm she had had to put up with from Simon. He thought they were an item and she refused to get near him physically. He put it down to the fault of his wife, Paula, that she hadn't cleared out earlier. He couldn't accept she didn't fancy him, and wanted to experience freedom for herself. Hailey was starting to like the idea of being independent, if only Simon would leave her alone.

The doorbell rang. Hailey peered into the hall and could just see the outline of him through the frosted glass of the front door.

'Would this weekend be OK?' Hailey asked. She wanted a break from Simon's constant badgering. He refused to believe that she had not been waiting longingly for her chance to be with him.

'Actually, Hailey, I was hoping you'd come for more than a weekend. There really is so much to do and I'm still finding my feet at work. I need your advice.' There was a pause.

'No, you need my body to do the running and get things organised, be honest, Kate. You've given up on my advice. Didn't you say that we'd outgrown each other?' Hailey had not meant to be so blunt but Simon had rung the bell again. His presence was becoming a threat in itself.

'Hailey, don't sound like that. It's not like you to be bitter or anything. I trust you, I know your judgement is good . . . please. Could you not delay the start of your course by one week? We've so much to talk about and David is very busy with the new office. He's taking on new staff. Things have really begun to happen quickly here.' Kate sounded desperate.

Hailey watched the figure at her door and her own desperation got the better of her. 'OK, I'll come down Saturday and return the following one.' Hailey heard the sigh of relief in Kate's voice as she thanked her and said they would send her the ticket. She wasn't to worry about a thing, money was no object. Hailey would have preferred to say forget it but she was in no position to, so she told Kate to thank David for his generosity. After all, it's better to give than to receive she reminded herself, so she was doing David a favour — well, the thought made her smile before she took in a sharp breath and opened the door to Simon.

'I thought you were ignoring me,' he

grinned as he spoke.

'No, I was talking to Kate on the phone.' She gestured towards the telephone.

'How is the southern belle?' Simon could not talk about her without heaps of sarcasm or jealousy.

She had the feeling he did not care so long as she was miles away. 'Happy, in fact I'll be going to see her soon.' Hailey smiled broadly.

'When?' Simon's question was very abrupt and he did not smile back.

'This coming weekend and I'll be gone for a week, at least.' She saw his face drop. His mood changed abruptly.

'I'll look after the place for you, but leave an address so I can get you if anything goes wrong.' Simon was most persistent.

'Thanks, but it's only a week.' Hailey meant he didn't need to do anything, but as his face lit up she knew he had not taken it that way.

'Yeh, that's right, love, it's 'only' a week, no big deal, then Paula's visiting her sister for a week and it'll just be us two when you return.' He winked at her, angering and worrying Hailey further. 'We could hole up together. Make our own little love nest.'

'Simon, there is no 'us', there is not going to be an 'us', there never should have been and there will never be, please believe that. We will not be holing up together, can you understand that?' Hailey was speaking in a low controlled voice because she didn't want the neighbours picking up on Simon's advances.

'Hailey, you'll see. It will all be fine, we'll sort things out as soon as Paula's left, only three months now, then you can relax.' He leaned forwards. 'No need to worry what the neighbours think then, eh? That's what I say. We'll even remarry in your church. They're OK about second timers aren't they? So it will be all legal like. You'll see, Hailey, it will be just what any young bride dreams of. You won't be disappointed with me.' He winked at her to stress his point. Hailey stared and cringed at his touch.

'Simon, I've got to go. Excuse me.' She shut the door, her heart sinking as she heard him whistling happily to himself as he sauntered up her garden path. The situation was becoming intolerable. She didn't love him or want him but he refused to believe her. The sooner she went to Kate's the better, only she'd stay a fortnight if they would have her for that long. All her plans were being thrown to the winds, but for the first time in her life she was thinking of moving herself. If he wouldn't take no for an answer then she would have to go. She couldn't exactly tell the police or anything. He hadn't attacked her; he had the key to her house and had done jobs for her. There was nothing she could do. Hailey thought you don't get people in trouble with the police because they love you. No, she had to find another answer; she would find a live-in nanny job. There was a magazine that advertised them all the time. He'd never trace her then.

★ ★ ★

It was quite late in the evening before Billie agreed he was tired enough to sleep. Sarah was also tired and nervous, James realised, as she entered the living room with a file tucked under her arm.

'If you wish to turn in, this can wait. I mean, he would talk the leg off a donkey and I understand that you came here to rest yourself . . . '

'Relax, I'll guarantee that by the time we have gone through all of that your problem will not appear to be so bad and you will sleep peacefully at night again.' James took the file and spread the various papers out on the dining room table. He then pulled out his laptop from its case and sat there studying each form and letter in turn, intermittently tapping away at his keyboard. He reorganised them placing each carefully in his own preferred order. He was pleased that Sarah made him a pot of tea and left him to work at his own pace. He became James Hood the professional, with a keen business eye. He could see the skill and foresight of the man, George, and also the determination and effort of Sarah to try to keep the work going. What she lacked really was the extra funds to pay for the work that George had expected to complete himself. That was what was holding her back. But James could see how the venture would be a financial as well as moral success. More than that he could also see how to raise the extra funding for it and spread the word that the place was there. In short, he was exactly what Sarah needed at a point when she had been about to lose everything to some cunning entrepreneurs, who were forcing her hand to sell the property below its value and definitely well short of the potential.

'Well?' she asked nervously, when he finally looked at her and put all the papers back in the folder. He turned his laptop to face her.

'Well, I would like to congratulate you, Miss Reynolds. I think George would have been pleased with what you have achieved so far. However, now is definitely the time to accept help as offered.'

'Sell you mean?' She looked deflated.

'Absolutely NOT! No, I would keep to your plan, with a few minor changes and slight adjustments. The first thing you have to do is clear the arrears and keep the bank happy. Then you need an injection of funds to complete the work, and promotional planning. No problem, you'll be home and dry and very busy establishing yourself.' He smiled at her numbed expression.

'That's all very well to say, James, but you are forgetting one crucial point. I have no more capital to inject.' Her cheeks coloured, as much he suspected with the frustration as the emotional baggage the place held for her. 'Do I go to the bank and ask them for a loan to pay them back?'

'You accept a partner, who funds the extra you need, helps to coordinate the effort whilst leaving the day-to-day

92

management up to yourself.'

'Do I advertise in the press? It takes time to find such people and how do I know who to trust?' Sarah's response was definitely born of frustration and he forgave her the sarcasm.

'No, I'll draw up an agreement and, if it is fine with your solicitors, I'll inject the capital and be a 40% shareholder. I can not be here so it will have to be co-ordinated from here and London, which is not a problem fortunately, but first, Sarah, there is one question I must ask before I would put a penny in.'

'I don't have a criminal record or a bad credit rating,' Sarah offered, not understanding what he was about to ask her.

'Both of those things are easily checked, and I would before entering into any business venture. However, what I need to know is this. Are you committed to this? Was it George's idea and you are trying to fulfil his dream? I shall not invest even at this level unless you are committed wholeheartedly to it.'

'It was my idea. George was thrilled and saw the value of it, but the idea was mine not his. Yes, I wanted to do this and I still do.' She picked up her file possessively.

'Then would you consider my offer?' he asked.

'You believe in it, don't you?' she smiled at him.

'Yes, or I wouldn't offer. I'd help you sell at the best price instead.' James grinned back at her.

'Then tomorrow we should speak to the bank and the solicitor.' James shook her hand. To her it meant the realisation of a life's dream. To him it was a small investment that, handled well, could grow nicely, and an interest outside of the city. Tomorrow he would do something purely for himself — and of course for the boy, Billie.

6

James entered the office with a great deal of anticipation and consternation. It had taken a real effort to leave his new friend Billie. The realisation that he didn't have to return to his old life — that he could hop off the treadmill whenever he chose was as exciting as it was daunting. How was Blake going to take his news? Frankly, for once Blake's opinion held no hold over James. Now that alone was a liberating thought.

'James, and about time too. Five minutes late! That's not like you. Time's money, you know the motto. Don't let it become a habit!' Blake was flicking through a file by the window, behind his uncluttered desk.

'Yes, I'm fine. Good morning, Blake, how are you?' James asked, as he entered the room and stood opposite his boss, the owner of Phoenix PR.

'What?' He glanced at James and then tossed the file over his desk to him. 'No time for that now. I want you to take this one on.'

'Blake, there is something I'd like to discuss with you. I . . . '

'Yes, well you should have got here five minutes earlier then. Now, you're late and behind schedule. So read it, digest it and do a good job. It's not big bucks yet, but 'FITTS' is run by a good and old friend of mine, with some really solid ideas. Encapsulate them into hype, and hook this account. I want my percentage of his future. Don't blow it, Jimmy! I'd see to this myself but I have to fly to Hamburg. I'm relying on you, so don't let me down, not on this — it's personal and I've broken my own rules by allowing a friend into my business sights!'

'When have I ever?' James asked.

'Never, yet, so don't slack off now.' Blake looked at him and smiled. 'You've just had a holiday, haven't you?'

'Yes, that's partly to do with what I

want to talk to you about.' James looked up hopefully. He wanted to explain about how he'd felt, what had happened to him and what he intended to do with his own future.

'Yes, well we'll do lunch next week. Check with Mandy when I'm free — on your way out.' Blake picked up the phone, the meeting was over.

James left and waved to Mandy as she answered the phone and said, 'Yes, Mr Blake.'

James didn't wait around. He knew when he was being given the brush off. Whatever Blake thought he had been wanting to say he obviously had decided James would have to wait or was hoping he would forget it and deal with it himself. He returned to his office and gazed out of the window. Below the streets were filled with well-dressed office workers, bustling about, rushing to arrive at their next appointment on time. Five minutes late, that was all, for goodness sake! Had his life become so crammed that cost was now measured in five minute lots? What about all the things he could have said in that time? 'Blake, I'm quitting. Blake, I want you to listen to me, I have an idea, but it isn't one you will find appealing. It's not profit making, not for at least the first two years, and if it is, I'm not keeping all of the money.'

He ran his hand through his tousled hair and dropped the file on the desk. He read the brief to represent Mr David Penwick. He was to come up with the package — stationery design, image, adverts, but for an unusually low fee. Why? Would he do it for a friend? Did Blake still have any? It could be his last client, he supposed. It was hardly a multi-national. Then he'd have time to develop his investment on Wight.

The phone broke through his thoughts on his latest 'mission' into the world of image and materialism.

'Hi, lover,' the voice of Michelle almost sang to him from the other end of the line. Actually, he thought, that was where their relationship was going, but how could he tell her? He was not good at letting people down.

'Hi, Michelle. Can we do lunch together?' James asked.

'Sure can; your place or mine?' Her voice was an open invitation for him to have Michelle for dessert. That was the trouble, though; he'd changed, become bored, and needed more from a relationship than just kicks.

'A restaurant, where we can talk but where we're not distracted,' James said, hoping he wasn't making it obvious. Hurting people wasn't something he liked doing, but between Michelle and Blake his life had become one long, exhausting, meaningless mess — an existence where he had more money than he had hours in the day free to spend any, although Michelle tried hard to. Between them they seemed to have nearly gained control of his every waking minute. However, the last week on Wight had been so refreshing. Even though he had given money away he had not spent nearly as much as he would have had his original plan come to fruition.

'You're not going serious on me, are you lover?' She giggled girlishly and he felt his stomach knot.

'Meet me at Luighi's at noon,' James answered, trying to sound as if he were distracted, as usual, by work.

'OK. I'll manage without you, till then!' She was still giggling.

He put the phone down and stared at it. 'So how did your holiday go James?' He shook his head and stared blankly at the file. 'Onwards!' he muttered to himself.

★   ★   ★

'Hailey! Hailey!' Kate's excited voice drifted over the crowds of people milling around King's Cross station. It seemed smaller than she remembered it from a weekend visit years earlier, or perhaps it was just packed with more people.

'You look great, Kate.' Hailey hugged her and she meant every word of it.

Kate had a new short haircut. Her hair now sported blonder bits, which added to her new image. Wearing a smart suit and heeled shoes that accentuated her long legs and slender figure.

Hailey had travelled sensibly, packing only the basic necessities for an informal stay. She had her best jeans on, white sports tee shirt and a new navy fleece. Her trainers were also recent additions, but as her tastefully groomed sister and her expensively suited partner greeted Hailey, she had a feeling of being dressed completely inadequately.

David picked up her rucksack. 'This is it?' he asked her with a big broad smile. Friendly approach, thought Hailey, but as she looked into his impassive eyes, she wondered why they never seemed to be in agreement with his mouth.

'Yes, I thought I'd travel light,' Hailey answered, wishing she'd purchased the cheap wheeled suitcase instead of her rucksack.

'Well, we'll do lunch, then you two girls can go and have a browse around the shops and I'll meet you back home for dinner. Don't worry about a thing, Hailey. You're here as our guest and I don't want you to pay for anything.' David had his arm resting around Hailey's shoulders.

He's asserting who's boss, Hailey thought, as she listened to the confidence in his voice.

'Kate has a budget for the wedding, which includes your outfits too, so all you have to do is make her happy by finding yourself something beautiful to wear. I want only the best for Kate, and I know how much you do too.' He squeezed her shoulder tightly before releasing her as they approached the taxi rank.

Great, Hailey thought, I'm not even out of the station and already he has his master manipulation plan under way. Hailey opened her mouth to turn down his kind offer of free outfits when one would clearly do, when his mobile phone rang.

'Penwick, speaking.' Kate picked up

Hailey's bag and waited silently as he answered his call.

'Penwick' was being very serious, Hailey mused to herself.

'Yes, yes, but do you really need me now of all times? Mmm, I see, yes, you have a good point. Yes, well we better not risk blowing it. This is damned inconvenient, but I'll be there within the half-hour. Bye!' David turned to them wearing what Hailey could only describe as an overly apologetic expression.

'Oh, David, you're not going are you?' Kate pouted childishly at him.

'Sorry, Poochy. I just can't help it — business calls, they need me to make the decisions.' David gave her a kiss and shrugged his shoulders apologetically at Hailey. 'Sorry, Hailes — you understand how it is, don't you?'

'Oh yes, don't worry about us, we'll be fine. See you later,' Hailey answered, relieved as he was going. He was no doubt relieved that the 'girls' could now entertain themselves. 'Hailes' she ranted in her head — hailstorm if he's not careful.

Hailey was glad when a taxi drew up and she and 'Poochy' were deposited in it to be free to enjoy a 'girlie' lunch as David put it. Hailey was beginning to wonder if her stomach was up to this trip. She'd left the overbearing advances of her 'friend' Simon to find herself staying with the sickening off-shoots of the Care Bears, or so it seemed to her.

Once they were settled in a trendy wine bar with some pasta dish placed in front of her, which had an equally fancy sounding name, Hailey smiled at her sister. 'Well, 'Poochy', how's life in the smoke then?'

'That's just David's way. He likes his women soft . . . ' Kate blushed slightly as she looked reflectively at her wine.

'Yes, that was what I thought too. Tell me, how many has he got?' Hailey asked, as she tucked into her dinner, wishing the portions had been slightly more generous as she ate the one lettuce leaf that had been placed on her plate for effect, rather than nourishment.

'Just one! I'm enough for any man. But then David is not just any man. I was saying that he likes women to be soft and feminine. You know damn well what I meant, so don't start.'

The old Kate showed through the welcoming veneer, which put Hailey more at ease. 'Right, I'll try not to get under his feet too much then,' Hailey said dryly, as she pressed the plunger down on the cafétierre. 'I've always liked playing with these things,' she said, as she watched all the coffee grounds get pushed to the bottom.

'Honestly, you're like a child with a new toy.' Kate laughed at her. 'You'll be playing happily all day at home, that's for sure. David likes gadgets.'

'Sometimes the simple things in life give us the greatest pleasure. Speaking of which, how is life with David?' Hailey added and laughed at her own joke.

'You're naughty, Hailey. He's a great

guy. He has a certain old-fashioned charm about him, but he's doing really well and you'll really love the house. It's brilliant. We're going to be really happy there. He takes fantastic care of me, and lets me choose everything. He says I've a great eye for perspective and colour,' Kate boasted proudly.

'I agree. You'd have done fantastically well at university. You could have had your own business; interior designer for instance. Perhaps he will set you up in one and let you fly. You're bright and talented.' Hailey stared straight at her sister, who looked blankly back at her.

'But I want David . . . not a business, I love him,' Kate answered and, to Hailey's surprise, looked at her imploringly, as if seeking support not criticism.

'Yes, I realise that. I just thought that perhaps, as he is so well off, you could do both.'

Kate stared down at her plate and twiddled aimlessly with her pasta.

'So where are we going for this wedding dress then?' Hailey hadn't the heart for a battle. She was still reeling from the problems that had emerged with Simon and wanted to lose herself in Kate's world.

Instantly Kate's face lit up and for ten minutes she described in minute detail the dress she was already having made for her big day.

'So come on then.' Kate stood up.

'Where are we going if you've already sorted your stuff out?' Hailey asked as she followed her through the restaurant.

'To sort you out, and I don't want any objections. It's time you stifled that working class pride of yours and lived a little. You're our guest and that means we will treat you and we will pay for your stuff and have no arguments — better to receive so that others can give, remember? See, my Sunday school lessons paid off.'

Hailey was about to complain bitterly at being told what she should do when a beautiful blonde woman, sitting at the table she was about to pass, suddenly stood bolt upright. In a split second, she leaned purposefully across the table and tipped a glass of red wine into the lap of the man sitting opposite her.

'That's what I think of your stupid decision. Is it clear enough for you, James? If the stain's too embarrassing, ask God to turn it back into water!' The woman glanced towards the ceiling then stormed off leaving her embarrassed 'friend' staring up at Hailey.

She quickly grabbed two cloth serviettes from the next empty table and offered them to him.

'That went well,' Hailey voiced her thoughts out loud and could hardly believe her ears as she spoke. She put her careless words down to embarrassment.

'Actually it went better than expected, I'm still breathing.' The man tried to grin as he dried his trousers. 'Thank you,' he said to her as he quickly dabbed feverishly at his lap. Heads that had turned and stared at him were now returning with smug grins to their dinners.

Hailey paused. 'You're welcome. I

didn't mean to make light of it — whatever it was.' She felt sorry for him, but followed after Kate. He grabbed his leather jacket off the back of his chair, held it in front of his stained trousers and walked to the counter to pay.

Hailey joined Kate outside the restaurant. 'Hailey, that was none of your business. Ignore stuff like that here, or you could find yourself with heaps of problems. Besides, you don't know what he's done to her, the rat!' Kate was flushed red and had obviously sided with the blonde.

'How do you know he is the one who has done anything? It was her who was being aggressive; all he was doing was talking to her.' Hailey raised an eyebrow at her sister.

'Easy to say that, but it was what he was saying to that poor girl which made her do such a thing.' Kate looked pointedly at her.

'I don't know that. I wasn't listening to their conversation,' Hailey answered but she had observed the body language as it built up to the blonde's overreaction.

'She must have been really provoked to act like that in public.' Kate hadn't seen the man step out of the restaurant behind her.

Hailey tried to warn her he was there. 'Lower your voice, Kate.'

'You don't know what the rat has done to her; a woman doesn't react like that in public without provocation. He's probably a ba . . . '

'Actually, she was provoked.' His voice made Kate jump, but Hailey couldn't help but grin at the impish, yet confident air of the man. There was something about him that didn't seem to be the stuff of ba . . . rats, yet she couldn't explain what it was. 'Excuse me, ladies.' He calmly flagged down a taxi and swiftly departed.

'What a cheek! Did you see that? He even nicked our taxi! Told you what he was didn't I? — a selfish 'B', poor lass. Anyway, let's not let a male chauvinistic pig spoil our day. You don't know him. James puts James first and foremost every time.'

'James — you know him? How?' Hailey was surprised, but then it was unusual for Kate to care so much about other's discomfort when her head was full of her own plans and problems. Hailey thought she should have realised.

'He works for Phoenix PR, and we're blessed with his services.' Kate turned her lip back as she spoke, and then flagged down the next taxi. Hailey wondered which member of the opposite sex sprang to light when the term 'male chauvinist pig' was mentioned in front of her — David perhaps? More than the stranger with the wet pants, Hailey thought. She also wondered how she could meet this James again through the weak link with David's company. She didn't fully understand why, but she continued to think about him throughout the day.

Three hours later and Hailey was

duly 'sorted'. She had her wedding outfit, plus slacks, tops and new jacket. Once in the department store there was no stopping Kate. She had a gold account card and everything went on it. Within the first day of being in her sister's new life, Hailey felt as though she had been purchased as part of the wedding package.

The biggest shock was being taken to a trendy hair stylist and losing the heaviness of her bob to a more fashionable long-layered look. Even Hailey had to admit it suited her, taking at least five years off her looks, or was it just that she now looked her real age instead of a more mature woman. She nearly fainted when she heard the cost of the restyling as Kate insisted on paying.

Hailey's biggest surprise came when she saw their house. She loved it. It was just as Kate had described it and so near to the sea.

Hailey curled up on the guest room bed amidst sheets edged with Italian lace and a duvet so light she could hardly feel its weight only its warmth. It felt almost pleasing to her that David was looking after Kate so well. If this was a cage, it was an extremely well gilded and comfortable one. Hailey reached out and picked up an envelope that had been left for her on the bedside table. The card inside was beautifully embossed with all the details of the wedding. They'd even had a special invitation printed out for her. Then her eyes rested on the date 25 May. That was only a month away.

7

'Morning, Sis.' Kate's voice was full of joy.

The light shone brightly through the highly polished windows and bounced off Hailey's less than beaming face.

'What time is it . . . 'Sis'?' Hailey asked, wondering why she was feeling so tired still.

'6.45 a.m.' Kate sounded so awake that it made Hailey feel even worse.

'Kate,' Hailey looked at her sister who was already dressed in a pair of black trousers and an oyster coloured silk shirt, 'are you going somewhere?'

Hailey sat up in her pink pyjamas with two white poodles printed on the front of them.

'No, well not just me, we are.' Kate tugged the duvet off Hailey revealing the bottom of her pyjamas, which had little poodles all over them. 'Very sweet, I'm sure, if not a little tasteless.

Definitely not sexy.'

'They were a fiver in Kenzie's in Dean Street; and before you ask, no I don't want them replacing. They're very comfortable, regardless of taste. My style is comfortable! Where are we going at this time in the morning? We've done the shopping and who will be open now anyway?'

'This is the land of the commuter. We live out of the city and commute into it. So move it!' Kate opened the door to the en suite.

'You sound like . . . '

'You! Frightening, isn't it? David has achieved in less than a month what you tried to do through my whole life. What does that tell you?' Kate opened the built in wardrobe door and pulled out one of Hailey's new outfits.

'It tells me you're desperate to impress him and not being your true self.' Hailey crossed her arms around her knees as she hugged her legs to her chest on the bed. 'Or did you expect me to cry — I failed?'

'Actually, I thought you might just admit it shows David is good for me, but I can see I'm going to have to open your eyes further. I'm taking you to the office, show you his new business, and my own office,' Kate paused for a moment to allow herself a broad self-satisfied grin, 'and introduce you to Frank, his partner. He's single — well, recently divorced, but really nice and . . . '

'Not interested, thanks all the same, but I'll gladly come and view your office. Do you manage to keep it tidy too?' Hailey's thoughts returned to Simon. She had not left him the spare keys, nor had she given him Kate's address. She'd popped a note through his door just to say she would be with Kate and not to worry about the house. There was nothing worth stealing in it anyway. She hadn't told him when she would be back. Just that she might stay on if things went well. She'd suggested he forgave Paula and try for reconciliation; after all, he was far from blameless himself.

'You should be.' Kate's voice continued.

'I should what, sorry?' Hailey rubbed her eyes and stretched out then stood up focussing on the new day.

'Be interested in men, because you're not yet thirty, but time is marching on and while you've got the goods you need to . . . '

'Sell them?' Hailey looked accusingly at her younger sister.

'No! That's not what I mean at all. A little flaunting wouldn't go amiss, though. Frank is only thirty-five; just right for nesting and starting a family. You'd like that. He has the big detached house at the corner of Warwick St and Elm. It's only ten minutes walk from here.' Kate was about to launch into what had obviously been a well-prepared lecture, when Hailey started laughing.

'What's so funny?' Kate asked.

'Is that what you think of me? Breed her quickly before she turns into a dried up 'spinster'? Crikey, you've only just fled the nest. I haven't decided yet what I'm going to do with my life.' Hailey's laugh stopped and her smile disappeared. 'Besides, if he is just right for nesting time, why did he divorce?' She was having enough problems trying to establish her own space back in the north, because of Simon's perpetual attentions, without being badgered by Kate down here. It was her own life now, but it seemed that, even though Kate had deserted her, she thought she could still orchestrate it for her. Hailey now viewed Simon, not as a friend, but more of a predator — waiting to pounce as soon as he had the chance. 'I could see the world. I'm considering options and I'm applying for a passport.'

'With what? That takes money.' Kate laid out Hailey's clothes for her on the end of the bed. 'You can borrow my make up.'

'I'll use my own lippy thanks. Besides, there are ways of working abroad without having to pay to travel around it,' Hailey answered, as she disappeared into the en suite. She couldn't help but curl her toes in the shag pile rug as she walked over it to the tiled floor of the bathroom.

'Stay here. Let Frank court you. He's got loads of money and he's looking for a nest builder not a career woman or good time girl. I've told him all about you and I think he's really interested. If you play your cards right, you could hook him. I know you could — with a bit of effort. Besides, if you go fruit picking around the globe all you'll see is a few trees, lots of creepy-crawlies and have an aching back for your trouble,' Kate said sarcastically. 'You don't like flying, anyway,' Kate shouted through to her.

'How do I know? I've never tried it. No, I'm considering doing temporary mission work, giving people — you know the real missionaries — holiday relief, that sort of thing. Well I'm looking into it anyway. Thanks for your vote of confidence that you would do a sales pitch on behalf of your poor lonely and pathetic sister — not!' Hailey shoved her toothbrush into her mouth as the bathroom door flew wide open.

'You can't.' Kate's figure appeared in the doorway. Hailey saw her in the bathroom mirror. Her body language told Hailey she had really shocked her. Do her good, she thought.

'Why ether mot?' Hailey continued brushing her teeth, whilst trying not to laugh at the response she had triggered in her sister. At least, Hailey thought, she had had the courtesy to mention an idea to her before arranging her own departure! 'I can do what I want, just like you did.'

'You'll get malaria or something awful from the water. Don't be ridiculous. You can't leave. Hailey, you do like men, don't you?'

'What?' Hailey's voice was sharp. She spun around resenting the implication and the attack on her personal life.

'You heard what I asked.'

'For the sake of our relationship I

don't think I heard correctly! Besides, if it's a futile attempt to get me to fall at this Frank's feet then you're wasting your breath.' Hailey felt a stab of pain at Kate's comment — if only she knew about what she'd been through because of Simon, and how she feared him.

'Sorry, Hailey, but I'm desperate. You're needed too much here.'

Hailey rinsed her mouth and was about to respond in kind when she heard the tone change in Kate's voice. What had started out as a joke had hit on something else by accident? What was underlying this whole charade of perfect bliss? Hailey sensed that 'Poochy' was not as happy as she had pretended to be.

'Why am I needed here? You have your new life. David is so good for you, your house is lovely and your wedding is planned. You're even going to show me your office, so what is it I'm so desperately needed for?'

'I'm pregnant.'

'What! I'll say one thing for you.

When you make your mind up, you waste no time. Most people take a few years to establish themselves first. You just plough right in. Does the office have a crèche attached?' Hailey dried her face and turned to her kid sister to see her in tears. Those words echoed in her mind again — stupid little fool. Hailey felt guilty for even thinking them, but if only Kate had told her about David before he had hooked her she could have opened the girl's eyes wider — perhaps. Well, she would have tried to, anyway.

'So what is your plan now?' Hailey gave Kate a tissue. 'If it involves me, can I suggest that you tell me, now? Please do not omit anything. You dropped David on me. Don't ever do anything like that again. I at least deserve to know what the hell is going on here if you intend to drag me into it.'

'David is delighted.' Kate sniffed.

'That somehow doesn't surprise me,' Hailey said blankly.

'I told you he's a really caring guy. He'd have a fit if I asked to have an abortion,' Kate snapped out bitterly.

'He's not the only one.' Hailey paled at the thought. 'Do you want one?'

'No, but I want my office and my job.' Kate looked up at Hailey, wide-eyed. 'This wasn't supposed to happen until he was nearly forty. I don't know how it happened.'

'Well, I suppose . . . '

'You know what I mean, Hailey. I'm on the pill. It shouldn't have happened.'

Kate was indignant.

'Lot's of women go back to work. He has bags of money and you can pay for a live-in whatever.' As Hailey spoke she couldn't believe the image that was forming in her mind. It was one that was to be one hundred percent accurate as Kate launched the proposal.

'Hailey, David said he wants me to be a full-time mum, but I'm not ready for that. I'm just not right for it. But he is willing for me to go back to work so long as we have someone to look after the baby who we really trust. The only person I really trust is you, Hailey, please?' Kate held Hailey's hand. Hailey could feel it trembling. 'I'm really scared. I don't have a mum to turn to, but I have you, Hailey, and I'm going to need a lot of support. David is still setting up the business and he's not around for days sometimes. Please stay here. We'll pay you as if you were employed here. It would be a whole new start for us all. Besides, it's what you've been training for, isn't it?'

Hailey looked at her. How could she begin to explain the sickness she felt in the pit of her stomach for her own loss, for the crushing sense of a newfound freedom, her hopes and dreams being wrenched from her grasp? She had contemplated being a nanny for a short time only, putting her own thoughts and emotions on hold until she found out more about the overseas work. Yet looking at Kate as tears dripped onto her silk blouse, how could she desert her or the unborn child? Yet, the hypocrisy of the girl was amazing.

'I'll think about it, but it will take some serious working out before I'll commit myself to anything. Besides, I have a home in Ebton, remember. Once I let that go and move here, what happens if you change your minds?' Hailey thought fleetingly of Simon, but was trying hard to say yes, not just out of a desire to escape from him. 'Go get changed. We've got an office to see and then we'll talk later. Kate you have to realise that for the first time I have a life of my own to fill. I don't need to permanently look after others. I might actually like to look after myself for a change.'

She watched her sister go with a whispered, 'Thanks.' Hailey could only think of what was another mess she was being dragged into, and decided she really must make more time to pray.

8

The office, though minimalist, impressed Hailey, Green plants brought natural energy into the place, Kate told her. She met the partner who eyed her with great interest and she noted a quick exchange of knowing glances between him and David. Hailey's hackles rose; she was not going to conveniently fit into David's clique; too convenient, too restrictive and claustrophobic. They may be ready to settle down but Hailey had just discovered how to think for herself.

- Fortunately, an urgent call interrupted proceedings and she was abandoned to the client waiting area where she was given a fresh cup of coffee and Kate promised to return to her shortly.

Hailey stared out of the window watching the city beneath. It looked like a sea of suits all rushing here and there. Not the sea she was used to, though.

There was a movement behind her and she suddenly realised that she was not alone.

Hailey had intended to sit down in the smart leather chair and read one of the boring magazines on offer, when their eyes met, both almost froze.

'You're the man in the restaurant . . .' Hailey started to say but realised mid sentence what a mess she'd made of it.

He grinned broadly, smartly dressed in his designer jacket, although his dark brown hair had a slightly unruly, escapist tendency, which made him look more human than the perfect coiffure style she had seen in the office.

'Actually, I'm the man in the waiting room, right here with you.' He was teasing her and his eyes seemed to glisten with life as he placed his portfolio onto the low glass coffee table. 'I was, I admit, the man who was deeply embarrassed by his 'ex'-girlfriend in a restaurant, yes. I'm glad that you recognised me without the soaking wet lap. I don't think I'll ever forget your kind face and the speed

at which you supplied me with dry nap-
kins.' He looked at her with a sincerity
that touched Hailey, although there was
an element of humour in his words.

'Sorry for stating the obvious, I just
got a shock when I saw you standing
there. It's a small world, isn't it?' Hailey
sat down holding tightly onto her coffee
cringing at her use of the age-old cliché.
She didn't like to set the cup down on
the highly polished glass table, as there
were no drink mats. She supposed they
would be too old-fashioned for such a
trendy place.

'Where, in the restaurant with a
damp lap or here?' He sat back relaxed,
enjoying her discomfort, yet, he had an
open manner about him that she could
not quite describe, but felt he was being
genuinely friendly.

'Here, I mean. You seem to have recov-
ered well — has she?' Hailey did not
mean to be intrusive, but they seemed
to have engaged in some kind of banter.
Both smiled at each other, both teased.

'I think she will have found another

victim by now.' He looked at the clock, a strange metal contraption with two pointers and nothing else on it to defile its pure face. A bit, she thought, like the people in the office that Hailey had seen, stylish but totally impractical. The face opposite her glowed with life, though, and a little mischief. Hailey realised to her surprise she was totally attracted to him, but then ridiculed herself, because he was tall, dark and handsome. She was short, plain and her normal mode of clothes was impover- ished compared to his attire. What he was seeing just did not reflect the normal 'her'. No, he must just be bored and was merely humouring himself with her whilst he awaited the next appointment in his busy schedule.

'I'm early for my appointment for a change,' he commented to himself and relaxed back into the chair. 'I'm James, James Hood and I would like to thank you for your quick thinking. Now let us put it behind us and move on to our present.'

'Don't mention it. I'd do the same for anyone.' Hailey warmed to him. Despite herself, she felt quite young for once with her new image.

'But your friend wouldn't, not for a bas . . . ' he looked around the room as if searching for the word, 'What was the term she was going to use again?'

'She's my sister, and I forget the exact term, but perhaps 'rat' would do. She possibly jumped to the wrong conclusion?' Hailey raised a quizzical eyebrow at him.

'Why didn't you then, Miss . . . ?' His smile dropped and his earnest expression touched her once more.

'Because . . . ' she leaned across intending to place her cup down on the table, almost lost in her thoughts; how could she tell him it was because she trusted him for some insane reason, then there was the conversation she had overheard, ' . . . I'm an impressionable sort of girl and the impression I was getting of you made me think you had known who your parents were.'

'Then you have excellent skills of perception and for that I'm very grateful. I'd gladly take you for a drink when I'm done here and say sorry to you properly. I'm usually very well behaved, I promise.' He smiled at her.

'Hailey . . . Sorry to keep you waiting.' Kate's sudden interruption made Hailey jump slightly; the cup in her hand slipped and spilled onto the table. Hailey grabbed the cup. James snatched up his portfolio and the offending coffee splashed over the shimmering table top. Kate squealed as she stared at the cream rug on which the table stood, but James dropped a bundle of tissues into the liquid's path stopping its flow.

'Well done!' Hailey exclaimed, her cheeks flushing with embarrassment at her own clumsiness.

'A favour returned in kind,' he replied, with more than laughter eyes.

Kate looked at James, her face already darkened at the near spillage positively glowered at him. Hailey watched the pair of them and didn't know whether to laugh or cry as James grinned sheepishly at her younger sister. 'I never travel without them . . . now.'

Hailey laughed out loud.

'Hailey, come on, I'll find Lucy and get her to clean up the mess.' She looked at James, with barely an effort to disguise her dislike of him. 'I'll tell Mr Penwick that you are here. Although, I shouldn't think he'll be in a hurry to see you after dropping an account just before its launch. It is highly unprofessional!' She turned abruptly and left.

'Sorry,' Hailey mouthed to him and wished it was he that she was leaving with. There was something refreshing about him that some deep part of her responded to instinctively.

'Don't be,' he said calmly and walked around the table to her, 'She's right. I would never have pulled out from a client at this stage in the game, but when my partner heard what I wanted to do, things turned rather ugly very quickly. We decided I should leave sooner, rather than later.'

'What ever could you have done that is so bad, that people have turned against you so easily?' Hailey asked before she thought about how intrusive such a question was.

'In a sense, I suppose you could say, I got faith. At least my faith in human kindness has returned, slightly.' James mimicked an American voice, but she knew he was serious by the commitment in his eyes. 'Certainly I rediscovered a faith I thought was long gone. A conscience is a bad thing to have in my job, it complicates things.'

'Hailey! The taxi is waiting.' Kate's voice echoed around the doorway.

'Duty calls, I wish you . . . ' Hailey walked to the door.

'Luck?' James's voice was almost cynical.

'No, well in a way, I wish you well, James Hood. Keep your faith.' She left without looking back at him, but wishing she could have stayed longer to find out more about the stranger with the wet lap from the restaurant.

★ ★ ★

Hailey arrived back at Ebton, still undecided as to where her future lay. True, David had made the move sound like a huge opportunity for her. She'd have her own en-suite room attached to the nursery where little Kate or David would sleep blissfully in the knowledge that his aunt was easily on call. If she didn't say yes, then they would have no choice but to employ a nanny. They'd rather she benefited from the salary of one, and share their home. They had even offered her the going rate. Then they could concentrate on the all-important building up of the firm for junior's future.

Why was there a huge niggling doubt in the back of her mind, if this arrangement was to be as perfect as they said it would be? She couldn't move permanently in before the birth.

She stopped by her door, fumbling to find the right key. Then there was James. But if he was leaving his company, then she would not be likely to meet him again. Hailey wanted to and yet it made no sense to her at all. He was a stranger whom she had only met on a couple of very unusual occasions, yet she wanted to know him.

Simon's voice startled her and she dropped the bunch of keys onto the floor.

'The prodigal returns at last.' He smiled nervously at her, then stepped over the small fence and picked up her keys before she could herself.

Hailey was balancing her rucksack in her arms, and her new small suitcase with its own wheels. David had insisted she have one for her next visit. It was packed with her new clothes, except her wedding outfit, which she had left in their house.

'So how did the wedding go off? Are they in the Bahamas now sunning themselves?' Simon asked sarcastically, obviously not caring a toss, and riddled with jealousy.

'Hi, Simon.' She reached out to take the keys off him but he masterfully took control, opened the door, grabbed her rucksack and stepped in first. There was no way he was going to be left on the doorstep this time.

'So how did the wedding go?' he asked again.

'It will be expensive, boring and artificial, but it will go fine very soon, but not yet.' Hailey headed straight for the kettle. It seemed as natural as anything to make a warm drink as soon as she returned home.

'Want one?' she asked sharply, but all she really wanted was for him to go and leave her alone. Hailey had thought she knew him, but all these years he had never believed a word she had said to him. He had put down her reticence to the presence and responsibility of Kate. So he'd waited and watched like a lion — no, a vulture, ready to sweep down on her at the first opportunity.

'Yep, thought you'd never ask,' he chuckled, and smiled at her, but she ignored him. 'So what now, lass?'

'I go back within the month for the wedding, and then I don't really know. I've so much to think about, so much to decide.' Hailey sighed then cringed as he wrapped his arms around her. She could feel the need in him. His grip was firmer, his kisses more urgent. He turned her to face him almost lifting her bodily against the kitchen unit. She tried to pull away from him, but his lips found hers and he pressed his onto her lips. She wanted to scream; she could taste the stale cigarette smoke on his breath and all she wanted to do was escape.

Hailey tried to pull away from him. He'd been her friend; she didn't want to hurt him, but he just would not back off. Whilst one hand held her waist firmly the other pulled at the bottom of her tee shirt. Feverishly, he pushed his hand underneath, desperately seeking her body and with no sign of pausing until his fingers found their target. She brought her knee up so hard she heard him cry out in pain. He doubled up, holding his groin.

'Hailey, have you gone mad? You nearly crippled me!' Simon's face was red with pain and anger.

She grabbed a bread knife from the drawer. 'Get out of here before I call the police, Simon,' Hailey was shaking and shouting.

'What the hell's got into you? Don't you know it's me? We can do what we like now. Paula's gone! It's just you and me. I'll never hurt you, I never have. We've waited years for this. Come on, lass, stop your fooling around. You've teased me too long. I'll marry you, as soon as I get the divorce through, so what're you worrying about?' He was moving towards her again. 'I won't leave you like your dad, sister and mum. I'll stay.'

'Go! Go!' She was yelling almost hysterically at him.

'Alright 'ave it your way. Perhaps I

was a little bit, too soon. But you're doing me brain in, lass. I'll come back later when you're settled in again and we'll talk this through. You'll see it will be all right. Simon says he'll take good care of you and Simon'll keep his word. You don't need to be scared. I won't stop for tea now. I'll bring a bottle of wine around after six. You'll be better then, you'll see.' He winked at her and went out whistling.

Hailey locked the door behind him and sank to the floor. The knife trembled in her hands and she watched it drop to the floor. She reached for the phone and phoned Kate.

'Hailey, you're back already?' Kate's voice brought an instant comfort to her.

'Yes. Listen, I've decided. I'll move down, but it will have to be soon. I won't have time once the baby's born to find my feet so I want to come down now and really get to know the place, OK?' Hailey was trying to sound calm but knew her voice was too fast, betraying her.

There was a sudden pause. 'I suppose that's great. Hailey, are you all right? You sound a bit funny.' Kate was concerned about her.

I must sound bad, Hailey thought. 'I'm fine. Look, I'll make some phone calls and arrange things here. Can David lend me the fare down?'

'No problem, Hailey. How soon do you want to return?' Kate's voice was filled with suspicion.

'No time like the present. I'll be out of here tonight. I'll book into a hotel near to the station and meet you at King's Cross tomorrow. I'll ring once I'm at Peterborough. I'll confirm once I've got my ticket. I just need to sort out some things. First time I'm glad I never kept any old junk. My things won't take long to sort out. There's a gaping hole here where your stuff was anyway. I thought I might decorate, but no need now.' Hailey's voice was firm but emotionless.

'Ask Simon to keep an eye on the place.' Kate's was the logical suggestion.

'No!' Hailey answered sharply, surprising even her. 'I mean he's in the process of separation. I don't want to bother him.'

'What's happened? Something's wrong, Hailey,' Kate persisted.

'I really miss you, that's all,' Hailey lied, but she knew it was the only one Kate and her ego would believe unquestioningly. Hailey would just have to live with the consequences of it.

'You twit. Get yourself down here and we'll pay the hotel. I'll book you into the Hilton or somewhere really nice — enjoy! Phone us from King's Cross when you arrive and I'll give you the details.' Kate hung up and Hailey knew she had made her a very happy person, but as the tears poured down her face she brought down two large old suitcases from the loft. She packed up everything that she owned or wanted to keep. The only thing she left was a stereo, television and a sewing machine neatly stacked in the centre of the living room. Kate's room was already empty.

Now Hailey's was also. The loft had been cleared after her mother died. She had collected memories. Kate and Hailey had swept through the house until only their present remained. She turned out every light in the house and went out the back as Simon knocked on the front door. By the time he'd tried the key and discovered the chain was on, she was already on a bus to the other side of town. She stayed the night at Shirley's place — a friend of hers from church, and did not return until Simon had gone to work the next morning. She knew he couldn't afford to miss a shift.

First thing the next day she phoned the furniture sales room, then the council, the Heart Foundation charity shop and lastly her friends. Three hours later everything was finalised. The bags and furniture had been collected, phone numbers exchanged and her future sealed. She had no home left of her own. Her spare keys were left with Shirley until they were collected. All her crockery and pans she gave to the church hall. Nothing was left. With her two heavy cases packed, she climbed into the taxi and headed into her future. She had just changed her whole life, and had no idea if what she was running to would be any better than what she was running from. A familiar voice inside her head said, *Oh yes it would be!* Besides, there was a chance, just a slim chance, that she might meet the man, James, again.

9

James wasn't looking forward to having a meal with David. He knew he was one of Blake's mates and that made it worse. Blake liked the company of shallower reflections of himself; if they were smooth, well off and greedy, all the better in Blake's viewpoint. He had hoped for a clean break from the company and to do some freelancing. However, Blake could be very persuasive once he regained his composure.

The phone ringing continuously interrupted his thoughts.

'Hi, lover.' Michelle's voice was smooth, almost purring. The image of her as a slinky Siamese cat crossed his mind.

'You like your 'lovers' covered in red wine?' he answered dryly.

'Oh, you're not still sulking about our little tiff are you?' She deepened her voice slightly which he found annoyed him even more.

'Why, aren't you?' James knew her too well to fall for her sweet words. She had been promised something — a new dress, jewellery, whatever, by Blake to win him back over. He obviously thought that David alone may not succeed.

'I'm not one to hold a grudge, James, you know me better than that. Come around here and I'll show you how forgiving I can be . . . ' her voice tailed off as she waited for his response.

'Tell Blake my mind is made up, and thanks for the offer, but I don't think so, sorry.'

'Bastard!' the word rolled of her tongue easily.

The noise of the receiver being slammed down made him laugh. Perhaps he was one, but she was so obvious that he knew she would be all right so long as someone bought her a trinket soon.

He thought about David's sister-in-law, Hailey. She appeared to have a good heart. He had seen the same compassionate look in her eyes when Michelle gave him the wine shower, as he had seen in Sarah's when she tended to Billie and other children. What on earth was she doing with David and Kate? Her sister was more like Michelle — going for gold. He laughed at himself. He had been one of them until a short time ago, yet he felt now he had woken up to himself, he would never go back to his old ways. As he dressed to go to dinner, he couldn't help wishing he'd asked Hailey for her telephone number. He didn't want to get involved with anyone, but perhaps they could be friends — some wish. At one time he wouldn't have given Hailey a second glance. Yet Hailey was attractive in a natural unpretentious way and she had a depth to her that he wanted to explore. James looked at the mirror and for the first time in his life realised he was actually falling in love with someone he hardly knew — a concept so very alien to him, but it felt so strangely natural, and the novelty of it was exciting. He'd help out Blake with his friend's account and in the process discreetly find out more about her from him.

* * *

Hailey arrived at King's Cross station once more and was soon to find herself being met by David, himself. This she had not bargained for. She was moving into a different world — his, and it was unnerving. Part of her liked it, the attention and the new image, but it was a small part. The rest of her already pined for the beach, the sea breeze and her many long walks. Hailey was rebelling against Simon and at the same time playing straight into David's hands. His ambitions included placing her alongside her sister in the family home. It was a situation that couldn't and mustn't last; she knew that as soon as David moved the mobile away from his ear and smiled artificially at her. What on earth was she going to do now? Panic threatened to engulf her as the cold realisation of what she had just done hit her full force. She was homeless, and far from self-sufficient. Well, perhaps not quite homeless, but her new home depended on her fitting in with the 'David's' idyll. She swallowed hard and forced an equally false smile onto her own face.

'Hi, Hailes, great to see you again, and so unexpectedly soon.' He paid a member of staff to lift her two large cases onto a trolley and then they followed behind as he put his arm around her shoulders. Possessively or protectively — either way, she didn't care much for the gesture.

'I'm taking you to a hotel that the company uses because I have a meeting there later, but don't worry it's an informal one. So you shall not be deserted for dinner.' David steered her through the crowds and towards the taxi rank. She was trying not to shake, but she had never felt so lonely, so small and vulnerable in her life. It was a feeling that she hadn't been able to shake off since Simon launched himself at her. Strange that was how she was dealing with it. He had infringed the privacy of her body as if she had been strangely detached from it. What was the most frightening thing was he had believed he had certain rights and that she desired him. The image of Neanderthal man crossed her mind. A side-glance at David told her they were in some way similar. Perhaps, she wondered was it her? — was she being too choosy, but then she remembered James's genuine smile, the depth to his eyes and the sincerity he had shown. She had felt warm inside, drawn to him and Hailey knew who suited her and who did not.

Once in the taxi, David pulled the glass window shut behind the driver and sat confidentially back in the seat next to her.

'Tell me, Hailey, honestly. Why have you changed your mind so quickly about coming down here? You weren't so keen when you returned yesterday so what has happened to make your world turn around so soon?' He put a hand on her knee. 'You can trust me . . . you do know that, don't you?'

'I hope so, David, because you will be marrying my sister and I would hate to think you would in any way hurt her.' Hailey stared straight at him and for once his eyes lost their veneer. He moved his hand and grinned at her with honesty.

'This is our first chance to really talk together, isn't it?' He switched his mobile phone off and pocketed it, then stared at Hailey intently. 'Ask me what it is that you want to know and let's get this conversation behind us. It is long overdue, I feel.' He folded his arms casually but nevertheless defensively.

'You arranged events amazingly smoothly, David. I admire your skill and determination in manipulating and capturing Kate,' Hailey answered in a matter of fact manner.

'I'm not sure if you are compliment-ing or insulting me. Which one is it?'

'You intended to marry her, and start a family straight away. She didn't. She's not so stupid, so how did you manage that without her knowing what you did?' Hailey folded her arms and stared at him.

He beamed as if she had in fact complimented him. 'Well, Kate likes a tipple of champagne to celebrate and was remiss about taking precautions.' David shrugged his shoulders and half smiled.

'She'd have realised in the morning that she hadn't taken it — unless someone had removed it first!' Hailey's mouth dropped open as she realised that was precisely what he had done.

'You can't be that naïve, Hailey. You're more my age than hers, and besides, I thought you'd have been all for her having a good home, loving husband and a baby to rear.'

'But she wanted a life of her own first, a career and a future where she could use her talents to their full potential!' Hailey's voice rose slightly.

'She's a kid — a rosebud who needs to bloom. With me she'll be the best flower in the whole garden. I'll look after her. I do love her and I value her, and she'll have everything she could wish for. What more could a girl want?' David looked at her as if he actually wanted her approval. Or rather he did not want her open disapproval.

'In time she might want to be free, what then?' Hailey asked him honestly.

'She'll learn that you can't have everything in life when you want it. Everything has a price in this world, so what's yours, Hailey?' David raised an eyebrow at her.

'You can't buy me, David. Don't try!' Hailey snapped at him.

'You're a very special person. Kate's right. You're out of step with the world and our generation. You still have a sense of propriety and honour. I don't want us to live under the same roof and be at war with each other. My home is important to me. We shall be friends, Hailey. We'll talk again — in time.'

152

David's attention switched to the taxi driver as he pulled up outside the hotel. A man in a top hat opened the door and another took her cases inside whilst David paid the driver.

Hailey signed in and David paid the bill, of course, whilst she went to her room to change for dinner. She collapsed onto the bed, feeling quite drained and shattered. She had a lot of things to work out and fast. David thought he had her in his palm and, in a frightening way, he had. She was rapidly starting to dislike men — well, except the one who had so fleetingly crossed her path recently. Then she tossed herself onto her back and thought of him. Why hadn't she done the liberated thing and asked James for his telephone number. She laughed a sad empty laugh. The answer was only too obvious. He had everything — looks, money, career, vocation and a pretty, if not volatile, ex girlfriend. She had two suitcases and an uncertain future and a few distant, but good friends.

10

Hailey had chosen a pair of black slacks and a long v-neck, silvery grey wrap around top to wear. She had made her face up with the new make up set that Kate had given her for the wedding. Although outwardly she appeared confident, she was aware of a growing feeling of insecurity as she left the safety of her hotel room. Her life was taking on new twists and turns and it felt very odd — her fear of Simon, and her apprehension of David. She had just left her childhood home, her church and friends. What was she going to say to David when they met again? They had no common ground other than their relationship to Kate. Who was the businessman? Why had she been invited to join them for dinner? She hoped it wasn't his partner. A cold feeling ran down her spine; what would she do if it was Frank.

'Hailey, so sorry to keep you waiting.' David approached her with an air of confidence that this time even Hailey found comforting. He had a very expensive looking suit on, excellently cut and even she had to admit he wore it well.

'Please join us.' He gently cupped her elbow and escorted her into the subdued lighting of the lounge area. Each cluster of softly cushioned chairs was in its own little cordoned off area. The effect was one of almost giving each group of people their own living room space.

'Who is 'us'?' Hailey asked casually.

'You look lovely, Hailey. You have a marvellous way of understating yourself that really accentuates your natural beauty.' David was not looking at her, or leering. In fact his attention seemed to be entirely on leading her to where they were meeting the other person.

'Are you taking the..?' Hailey spoke before she had time to edit her thoughts. She was not used to flattery, especially not when it was so sweetly wrapped in eloquence.

'No, I'm not. I used to work on behalf of a fashion house and, believe me, I know someone who has natural style. Even more attractive when they don't see it themselves.' David looked at her and repeated, 'Believe me.'

David showed her to a set of chairs in the corner. She could only see a pair of men's shoes sticking out from under the table. Even they looked expensive.

'Thanks,' she muttered quietly, and was surprised when her comment was met with a chuckle.

'I believe you've met James briefly at the office. He's having a bit of a mid life crisis — a little early, I may add. He can't be beyond thirty-five and my friend, Blake, for whom he works, has asked me to try to knock some sense into his head. He's about to blow his whole career skywards.' His voice was low. 'If he does he'll never work in this city again. However, if he'll join us, our business could expand rather more quickly than even I had ever anticipated.'

'What of your friend Blake?' She looked at David, but he merely laughed.

'Business, Hailey. Some you win, some you lose.' He winked at her.

'You want me to try to change his mind somehow?' Hailey asked.

'My dear, learn to trust me — just a little. If you recall I had no idea that you were to rejoin us so quickly. You are,' he glanced around looking for inspiration, 'merely an unexpected bonus, a pleasure for us both to behold. But as you are here you can definitely help with your charm.' He smiled broadly at her as they approached. James stood up instantly.

His eyes glanced at David and then he looked straight at Hailey. They welcomed her by the way in which they lit up as soon as he saw her.

'Mr Hood, we have a way of bumping into each other unexpectedly.' Hailey sat down in the chair that David had moved out for her. She had been feeling extremely tired, but suddenly felt refreshed by James's warm welcome, coupled with the relief that he was not the partner Frank.

'Not literally I hope?' David quipped as he sat down, but Hailey noted the quick double take he made as James greeted her. He never missed a thing. A waiter approached their table.

'Would you like to order drinks, sir?' He looked at James who was the taller of the two men.

David answered straight away. 'Hailey, what would you like to have to drink?'

'I like a good fruity red wine,' Hailey answered and cringed inside because she usually bought the occasional bottle of her local supermarket's own brand and could not think of one specific type. Her mind just went blank.

David said something to James in French and James nodded his agreement in return, accepting the choice.

'That would be absolutely fine. I'm quite partial to red wine myself,' James answered, and winked at Hailey, who met his eyes with hers and smiled back at him. David ordered two bottles, 'to start with' as he put it.

'I'm delighted to meet you again, Hailey, but you really must call me, James.' He was talking to her, whilst David looked on.

'Sorry, James, I should have introduced you two properly. This is Hailey, my sister-in-law, and Hailey, this is James, soon to be my director of marketing.' David's smile broadened as he noted the look of surprise on James's face. David laughed when James raised his eyes heavenwards at the suggestion.

'David, you are incorrigible. Blake set me up tonight so that you could dissuade me from leaving Phoenix PR, and you blatantly head-hunt me. That is not at all honourable — but, I have to admit, very enterprising,' James stared back at David, but his facial expression had hardened. Hailey thought it was like a veneer cast over his natural relaxed manner that he showed to her.

'Now you know the game. We're in business, James, not the girl guides. Blake thinks he needs you — but I know I need you.' David emphasised how serious he was by stressing the word 'need'.

The waiter returned to inform them that he had a table ready for them. So before the discussion had a chance to blossom any further they had to move. Hailey wondered if she had just been given the front seat in a sparring ring for two boxers about to fight it out. Or, if she had judged James correctly, she was about to see David bend over backwards to move a solidly deter-mined rock. She hadn't taken him for the kind of man who would be bought. From the way he dressed, she wouldn't expect him to need the money, unless he were just another of life's con men. She thought of Simon for a moment and was filled with guilt. For all his faults, he was not a con man. He would make some woman a dedicated hus-band so long as they accepted him and his way of life. Hailey couldn't — she didn't know what precisely she wanted — but she wanted more than he could give her. It was a shame he could not forgive his own wife the one indiscretion she had had and turn his attention back towards her. As she noticed the look in James's eyes she knew one thing for sure — she wanted much, much more than Simon could ever offer her and that it had nothing to do with money, and everything to do with life.

The conversation changed back to food and what they were about to order. David tried to suggest or manipulate everyone's choice, or at least that is what it seemed like to Hailey. She was used to buying and cooking her own food, not discussing one dish's attributes over another, particularly when half of them were not written in English.

'I'll have the chicken,' she pointed to the menu, 'that one, please.'

James, she noted, read out a slightly different choice when he ordered.

'So, James, are you interested in my

offer?' David beamed a smile at James who was searching for adequate words to express his thoughts, it appeared. 'You are, I can tell. We can discuss the terms and details later.'

'I'm interested, of course, David. However, I have given my word to someone very special, that I shall be available to help them with a personal project, and I will not break it.' James sipped his wine. 'Are you sure you can afford me?'

'She must be a very special person if this promise will cost you your career, your future and a very lucrative salary.' David watched James's reactions as he calmly put down his glass. 'I'm sure I can.'

'It is not just a 'she', it is a 'him' as well, a child, who deserves a lot better in life than he has been given, along potentially with up to twelve others. They are just the tip of a large iceberg.' James stared thoughtfully at his glass. 'It's not a decision I have made rashly.'

'Look, the world is full of losers and

only a few winners and there is no reason why a natural winner like you can't give to a good cause. With your lifestyle you can humour whatever whim you wish to without wearing sackcloth and joining forces with all the wannabes.' David gulped his drink, and Hailey felt a feeling of anger and resentment growing within her.

'What do you intend to do?' Hailey asked, sensing just how important these people were to James.

'They need cash and quickly; they also need a sponsor and someone who can help them raise their profile and own sponsorship in the future. I intend to take six months out of my schedule and give time to help them. I know it makes no sense to you, David, and I am not deserting my existing clients, but rather not taking on new accounts for the next few months, that's all. I also realise it is my life. Giving more back rather than taking all the time.' James was talking directly to Hailey.

'Then if it has been laid so clearly

upon your heart, you have no choice but to follow wherever it leads? Sometimes we have to do things that don't appear at the time to make sense to us, but money isn't everything,' Hailey answered, forgetting all about David's plan for her to talk James into joining him. 'Particularly when you already have plenty,' she added. Hailey wondered if she should have said the last comment but it was said before she had time to rethink her choice of words.

'Everyone has a choice. Why don't you give them some money? My company could be a sponsor and you could still work for us. In fact it would be a great promotional move.' David sat back, relaxed, obviously feeling that he had averted whatever crisis of con- science that had befallen James.

James shook his head, obviously not impressed. 'Let's enjoy our meal with- out the sales pitch. I'll think on it, David, but my mind is already made up. I shall not let them down.'

'Nor, would I expect you to.' David

filled up their glasses and James explained a little about Billie and Sarah, and Hailey listened wondering how old Sarah was. James seemed to admire her greatly and she suspected that this lady had hooked James without him realising it. She did not doubt, though, that he was the man for the job. For him to even consider such a volatile life change, she knew it had to be meant, but what of her own life and the changes she was making? Was that meant or had it been forced upon her, or had she panicked and acted out of sheer stupidity? Time would tell.

'So tell me something about yourself, Hailey. What brings you to the south?' James looked at her as she flushed, and hesitated. 'I thought you still lived 'up north'.'

'It's a long story.' How could she say she was running away from a manic obsessive friend to become a leech on her brother-in-law?

Again it was David who intervened. 'Hailey has kindly offered to come down here and help us set things up. So if you joined us, James, you two would be seeing a lot more of each other.'

Hailey realised that David would use anything and anyone, in order to get his own way.

'What a pleasant thought,' James replied, then he swiftly changed the subject.

By the end of the evening Hailey wanted nothing more than to follow James and help out with his new plan.

It was during coffee that Hailey's prayers were answered. David's phone rang. 'Excuse me, I do apologise for this.' He stood up and left them as he took the call.

'I think you should do what you feel is right,' Hailey said.

'I know you do.' He grinned at her surprised expression. 'So why don't you think I'm mad like everyone else around here does?' James asked.

'Because, there is a time to look at life through other values than just money and gain. I know it is not a commonly held view, but if you already have your financial independence, why not do whatever you want to do. Anyway, I'm not from around here,' Hailey answered honestly, having spent most of her life wondering how she was going to pay for things. 'Besides, I believe God sometimes presents us with situations we just have to get through to find out the true reason for it.'

'You follow your faith, that's good. I have a little faith too, but it has been buried deep down for so long I'd forgotten it was there,' James answered. 'I fell for the 'love of money' thing, instead of being grateful for having it. Michelle, the 'lady' I was with in the restaurant, was not at all amused when I showed her I was reassessing my original values.' James fiddled with the coffee cup in front of him.

'But Sarah is?' Hailey flushed red, as her question slipped out.

'Yes, Sarah is. She is devoted to her faith and the home she is building. She lives her whole life unquestionably by it,' James explained, his voice full of admiration for the woman.

Hailey realised he was in love with her and her earlier emptiness returned.

'Hailey, I . . . '

'Sorry, about that, David interrupted.' He didn't sit down to rejoin them. 'Listen, Hailey, I'm going to have to check out early in the morning. Can you make your own way back to our place?' He asked her the question as though he was telling her what to do.

Hailey answered, trying to sound confident, 'Sure,' realising she didn't know how she'd manage her baggage on her own, 'but I can't get the cases on and off the underground by myself.'

'Here.' David placed forty pounds onto the table in front of her. 'Take a taxi to Fenchurch Street and get on the Southend train. You can get a taxi at the other end to our place. We had this key cut for you.' He placed a house key on the table. 'Sorry to desert the two of you.' David bent over and kissed her cheek lightly. 'I'll see you tomorrow night, Sis. Speak to you soon, Jimmy, to settle things between us, bye.'

Hailey was left staring at the money in front of her on the table and she gritted her teeth. She felt humiliated. What would James be thinking of her. Was he a caring brother-in-law or was he paying for his latest purchase?

'The waiter will take the money as a rather generous tip if you don't pick it up,' James whispered to her. 'I should put it in your purse quickly before it is cleared away with the pots.'

She didn't move a muscle. James's hand covered the money and the key as he placed them into his pocket and walked around to Hailey's seat. 'Come on, he's so used to paying for people he doesn't realise how crass he can be.'

Hailey didn't say anything until they were through the lounge. Before she knew it, she was feeling fresh air on her face. The wine made her head feel as though it was a little light.

'No, James. I'm booked into that hotel. My room and bags are there,'

Hailey explained as they walked along the embankment of the Thames. It was a world away from her home.

'It's OK; I'm not whisking you away. I just thought you had something you needed to get off your chest,' he smiled warmly at her, 'and that a walk might do you some good.'

'I don't know you nearly well enough to get anything off my chest, Mr Hood.' She folded her arms across her body to hug herself against the cold breeze that travelled up the river, although, looking around her at the Houses of Parliament, the huge wheel and the hustle and bustle, she found so many distractions she hardly noticed it.

She felt the warmth, though, as James wrapped his jacket around her. 'James, remember.'

'Thanks, but shouldn't we go back inside somewhere where you won't get hypothermia?' Hailey asked him, as he shivered a little.

'Come on, I know somewhere we won't freeze.' He walked her down a

170

parallel street and into a pub. Nestled cosily into the back of the place, he sat her down and ordered two drinks.

'Why are we hiding in here, when we were already in a luxury hotel?' Hailey asked as she sipped her drink.

'Because in here we are not being observed, coerced, monitored or paid for.' He looked at her inquisitively. 'That is what David was doing. He manipulates and controls people. My apologies, if I'm insulting a close member of your family.'

'I know what he is and what he does. So the truth cannot really be an insult, and I hardly know him to describe him as 'close'.' Hailey nervously sipped the drink and felt the fear return to her as the reality of what she had done hit her hard. She could no longer return to her home. She'd given it up. Why couldn't she have fought Simon? Eventually she would have got through to him. If she was honest she knew only too well why. She had been scared of him ever since she let him sleep with her; just the once, but for the wrong reason; not for love but for reassurance and comfort at a time in her life when everything around her was changing and pinning her in. She wanted to be loved and had felt at her most desolate, but he hadn't loved her — not like she had imagined love would be. Instead, he'd wanted her, to possess her. She'd lived in a shadow of fear ever since.

'Why are you letting him control your life and fit in with his plan then? You are not at all at ease with him or his ways, are you?' James asked as if reading her thoughts, like the proverbial book.

In a moment of confusion she answered him honestly, 'I'm not. I've moved here and I've not even left a forwarding address.' Hailey's thoughts had been so much involved with Simon that she could only answer regarding him. Her head felt as though the wine had made it swim slightly. She was not drunk but as she saw the puzzled expression on James's face and the slow grin, she realised she had let a cat out of the bag; quite a big one. 'You mean David?' she asked him.

'Yes. I meant David,' he repeated. 'So who did you mean?'

'I must go.' Hailey tried to stand up, but James gently held her arm.

'Sit down, Hailey, please? Stop running away, there's no need to now, not from me, anyway.' He let go as she stared at his hand. Hailey sat back down.

'I left my home in the North East not to fall in with David's grand plan of happy families but because I had a neighbour, a friend who misread our relationship. I didn't want to cause either of us any more pain, so I took the soft option and ran. I'll go now that you can see what a complete wimp I am. It's been nice to meet you again, James. I wish you well with your venture and Sarah.' Hailey looked away nervously as she picked up her small handbag.

'It still is 'nice'. So tell me the complete story and let's see if we can put our heads together and try to help you out.' James's words were gentle and he watched and waited for her to respond to him.

Hailey looked into his deep brown eyes, hush puppy eyes she thought, and she realised how much she would like to put her head together with his. 'Why are you doing this? You hardly know me at all. You live a different sort of life to me. You could never understand mine.'

'Because, I like you — very much. I would like to know the real Hailey, not this person I keep bumping into. Tell me about him, this neighbour and what he did to frighten you so much?'

'I didn't say he did anything,' Hailey protested.

'I know you didn't, but I did.' James stared straight at her.

She couldn't understand what possessed her. Why on earth did she trust him, but she told him the truth about Simon. How a relationship had developed from a simple friendship and his position of guidance to a one night stand. One awful night which had resulted in an unexpected pregnancy and early miscarriage, leading to her silent pain and guilt. Not even Simon or Kate knew. She thought Simon had backed off, accepted that it had been a huge mistake, but he'd merely waited his time and the passing years had turned his desire into an obsession for her. James was right; she had never been so scared in all her life. 'So what do you think of me now?' Hailey asked, her eyes lowered, 'There is no need to answer that. I'd be grateful if you didn't share this with David.'

'I think you're an incredibly strong willed lady who hasn't had much of a chance at life. I also think that if you pick up Kate's offer, you'll never have a life of your own and you will be thought of as no better than the hired staff.' James was watching her closely.

'How can I let them down?' Hailey asked.

'You won't be. But she's let you down big time, hasn't she?' James asked and placed his hand over Hailey's.

'Yes. I've just told you I've left myself with nowhere else to go,' Hailey replied and saw a smile cross his face.

'No, not exactly. That is not true. You could stay at my place until we get things sorted out.' He squeezed her hand and gently kissed her cheek. 'It will work out fine, you'll see.'

Hailey stood up. 'What? Oh, I've been a fool once before, but not again!' She stormed off knocking the table. James's drink toppled over as he stood up to follow her. His trousers took the full force of it. He stopped momentarily to collect his jacket that had fallen to the floor and pushed his way through the crowd, and back to the embankment. There was no sign of Hailey.

'Damn!' He exclaimed and was annoyed by his poor handling of the situation and was frustrated as he had not meant to be insensitive. He could have followed her back to the hotel, but decided he had handled the evening badly enough already. He shoved his hands deeply into his pockets and walked towards the tube. He would just have to think of another way to approach her that could not be misunderstood. James felt the money in his fingers and the key that David had put onto the table for her. 'Oops!' he said, and smiled.

11

David was far from easy about his new sister-in-law. He didn't trust her and doubted she was as malleable as Kate thought she was. He had cleared a little time in his schedule and he was going to kill two birds with one stone. If he wanted things to go his way then he had to have knowledge. That was power. She had come south very quickly and if that was unlike her normal settled behaviour there had to be a reason for it. No one was going to live in his house unless he knew about their closeted skeletons personally.

He arrived early in the morning at Kate's old home. What a dump, he thought. He used her old key to go inside. Kate had been right, he thought, Hailey had run, and run fast. He went inside and saw a heap of electrical goods stacked in the middle of the old carpet. Oh, it was clean enough but, by God, he realised he had rescued Kate just in time.

The furniture had gone. A faded carpet was left around the deeper patches where the pieces had once stood. He went upstairs to find a sparse yet immaculately clean house. At least he thought his son would be well cared for. He never understood why people bothered to tidy up once they were leaving a place. Why clean it for someone else to put their own stuff in? But then he paid people to do that sort of thing anyway.

David's thoughts were interrupted as he heard steps running along the narrow hallway towards him. 'Hailey, I knew you'd come back to me. I . . . ' Simon bounded up the stairs two at a time. 'Who the bloody hell are you?' Simon asked, obviously bitterly disappointed.

'I might ask you the same question,' David said haughtily as he looked the dishevelled Simon up and down, taking in his old denim shirt, jeans and unruly hair; he even wore a pair of shabby old cowboy boots. All he needed was a sad Stetson and he'd be right for a rodeo, David thought.

'Listen pal, you get that smart arse out of here right now. This ain't your house, do you hear me?' Simon walked into the room facing up to David, who coolly stood there and stared back at him. He could smell the booze on the man's breath.

'You know Hailey . . . ?' David asked and he softened his voice as he spoke. 'Well?' He intuitively knew how to approach people to find out what he wanted. He thought it was one of his gifts — one of many that he prided himself on.

'Yeh, we're going to get hitched,' Simon said. 'So who the hell are you?'

'My name is Mr David Penwick.' He watched Simon's eyes lift up slightly and realised that, although he knew nothing of him, the man at least knew who he was. Hailey had more to her than he had envisaged. She certainly

180

was a dark horse if she'd managed to hide this dubious specimen of manhood from Kate. He was determined to find out all he could. No child of his was going to be brought up by anyone he did not consider suitable. This man was not that for sure, which raised a huge question in his mind over Hailey. He'd done the right thing by following his hunch and coming up north to find out why she had suddenly agreed to move. Besides, he had an ex wife who he needed to check up on. He might have enough evidence on her now to force her to drop the paternity suit. That would save him an ongoing expense he did not need.

'So you're the bloke who ran off with young Kate. Lucky bugger! Well me and you are going to be related soon.' Simon stood with his shoulders straight, only he was swaying slightly.

'So where is Hailey now?' David asked and saw the uncertainty rise in Simon's face.

'Well, she's been having a few cold

feet, like — with all the changes and that. It's been a bit much for her. So I'm just waiting for her to come back home, here to her Simon.' David looked around. 'She'll come back to her Simon, you'll see.'

'If we're to be related, and neither of us should really be here, then why don't we go to the pub and become better acquainted . . . Si?' David walked towards the doorway. He'd find out all he could from the fool and then he'd decide what action was necessary to take.

'Excellent idea, David,' Simon answered with enthusiasm as he heard the offer of a drink.

David watched him as he walked in front of him and down the stairs. 'I'll just get me jacket and keys. Back in a mo.' He sauntered out of the door and climbed over the fence of the next door's house.

The minute Simon had crossed the threshold David pulled out his mobile. 'Kate, tell me what you know about a rough cut called Simon.'

'He's our neighbour, or used to be, why?' Kate answered as the train took her to the office.

'Did Hailey and he have anything going between them?' David asked.

Kate laughed at the thought of it and then remembered where she was as heads turned. 'No, never, he helped out with jobs when things broke down but not with Hailey, not like that. He's married! They can't have anything going between them. I mean, there was nothing that I knew of. Can't be, not with Simon, no way! He's too old for her. Why do you ask?' Kate tried to keep her voice low.

'It appears he thinks they are an item. I'll see what I can find out from him. Keep it quiet, don't mention it to Hailey and I'll be in touch. Bye Pooch.'

David locked the door and the two of them climbed into his car. He drove them to a decent hotel he'd passed on the way in, which was a few miles out of town.

'Nice place,' Simon said as he walked in looking around. They headed for the lounge. Once plied with another drink, Simon was eager to tell his story — how he'd helped her over the years, how they'd fallen in love, but Hailey was young and she had her mother to contend with and then later, young Kate to support. He stressed how much it must have cost her, and David wondered if he was trying to get his hands on some money from him. Then he described how they crossed over the line and she had promised herself to him. His marriage was dead, finished. Then David had whisked Kate off to the south so nothing stood in their way. She had no right to put him through this anguish after all this time, he argued, after all he'd patiently waited for her. 'I'll put her right as soon as we're together properly. Once she's got this out of her system she'll be back where she really belongs, with me.' Simon slammed the empty glass down on the table.

'So when you last saw her, you told her what you intended for you both?' David asked calmly, watching Simon's movements as they became ever more animated, influenced by the alcohol.

'Yep.' Simon leaned in towards David, who tried not to breathe in the fumes. 'She needs a man. It's not healthy for a woman like that to be on her own, is it?'

David shook his head. 'Simon, you are a specimen of manhood from another time and place, do you know that?' he said dryly.

'Thanks, lad. Mind, that's not what my 'ex' used to call me.' Simon smiled a bleary eyed smile as he downed his last pint.

'Will you excuse me? I have to phone the office.' He placed a twenty-pound note on the table. 'Get yourself another drink, Simon, and take my advice. Forget about Hailey, she's no good for you.' David turned away.

Simon's eyes lit up at the sight of the

money and he swayed his way to the bar. 'She's the apple of me eye,' he said as he walked away.

David pulled out his mobile as he crossed the car park. 'Kate, I've seen enough. I'll finish my business here and then I'll be coming home. I'll see you later. When Hailey arrives, don't say a word about Simon. Leave that to me. I have a feeling she'll be glad to agree to my terms.'

'You said you'll give her a fair wage, David,' Kate reminded him.

'Oh, I think we're being more than fair, Pooch. Leave everything to David.' He laughed as he drove away leaving Simon in a hotel, half drunk and miles from his home. He loved the feeling of being in control, and people made such stupid mistakes.

* * *

Hailey checked out of the hotel and had her cases brought to the front as a taxi was summoned for her.

'Fenchurch Street station please?' she asked the taxi driver as the cases were placed inside.

She sat down in the taxi and was surprised when a familiar voice said, 'It's OK we're together.'

'James, what on earth are you doing here?' Hailey asked as he handed her the forty pounds and her key.

'You left these in my tender care.' James smiled that lovely inviting smile.

'I said all I had to say to you last night!' Hailey replied sharply.

'Well, I didn't.' James leaned forwards. 'I made a complete mess of it. I wasn't propositioning you. I just didn't put what I meant very well at all. So shall we try again?'

'Oh,' Hailey explained, 'I never thought you were . . . '

'Yes you did and with little wonder. I meant you could use my flat that was all. I wanted to offer you a part in the action at Green Gables.' James's eyes shone brightly with enthusiasm.

'How could I be involved? I have

little enough money as it is.' Hailey was confused.

'In my grand plan for it there is a need for more staff. You could help, if you want to. There wouldn't be a lot of money in it to start with but if I'm right you could have a regular job there. Start your life over.' He raised his eyebrows. 'Interested?'

Hailey's mobile rang. 'Hi Kate, I'm OK, I'm in the taxi . . . '

'Hailey, have you been holding out on me?' Kate's voice sounded cross as though she was having one of her strops. 'What have you been up to with Simon, and you'd better tell me the truth before David gets home.'

'I don't understand what you mean.' Hailey was amazed when Kate's excitable voice told her that David had found out about them.

'What! Is he checking up on me? Why? What a flaming cheek! He has no scruples.' Hailey's voice rose and James's expression changed from humour to concern as her face flushed with anger.

'No, he had to go up to sort out his ex and dropped by the old place before he came back,' Kate explained, her voice subsiding as Hailey's anger had grown. She rarely lost her temper but when she did it was like a volcano blowing.

'Why?' she asked.

'Well you did leave suddenly and now he's found out about you and Simon, then it's just as well, isn't it?'

'There is no me and Simon. There never has or will be a 'me and Simon' and if you want to know anything more about me, Kate — ask me, not David!' Hailey stared at James.

'OK, I am, aren't I? We'll talk about it later, but not in front of David, OK?' Kate's voice was now much calmer, almost placating. 'If there's anything I need to know you should tell me, though, because I'll look a complete idiot if David knows more about my sister than I do myself. He didn't want me to speak to you about it but Hailey you're my sister!'

'Then perhaps you should have talked to me more when you had the chance to, but that was something you failed to consider doing, wasn't it? Bye!' Hailey put her phone off before Kate could answer.

James looked at her and raised his eyebrows. 'What is it to be — a walk into another prison, with David watching over you instead of Simon, breathing down your neck all the time, or a walk of complete faith? David will try to manipulate you like he does everyone and you will be in his home. He won't pay you enough for you to leave. Come with me. Try a life of your own. At least until you really know what you want to do for yourself. I'm offering you a retreat — some 'you' time, that's all. They have not had the child yet; give yourself six months to find out what Hailey really wants in life. James wants you to be free, Hailey, not tie you down like those two.'

'You are amazingly persuasive,' Hailey said and grinned. 'Can you look after these two cases whilst I go and see Kate? I need to speak to her before

David arrives home.'

James took out a business card. 'This is my mobile number. Go see Kate and phone me when you are ready to leave. I'll pick you up, OK?'

'Tomorrow morning, would that be alright?' Hailey asked.

'Yes, I am returning to Green Gables in a week's time, just for a weekend, then I have things to attend to here. You can come and meet the team.' James smiled and he put his arm around her. She leaned into him, but then pulled back.

'What about Sarah? Won't she mind you bringing me home with you?'

'Absolutely not. The more help the better. She's a lovely person, she'll take to you on sight, I'm quite sure.' James was really beaming but Hailey's heart sank. Was this how Simon was feeling? He loved her, yet she could no longer be in the same room as him. Hailey was falling in love with James, but was he in love with this Sarah? There was, she knew, only one way to find out.

12

Simon, who had become increasingly annoyed and abusive as he realised that David had deserted him, was forcibly evicted from the hotel, under threat that they'd call the police if he tried to drive home.

'Fat chance, as I don't have a bleeding car!' he bellowed back at the bloke who had escorted him outside.

When the cold air hit him, coupled with the realisation that David had ditched him completely, he was consumed by a wave of anger that made him feel almost sober. He started walking back to town along the edge of the dual carriageway. In his mind he pictured what he would do to David when he tracked him down. What was his name? Fennon? Fenton? Fen . . . he stumbled off the kerb and had to pick himself up again. He staggered and almost fell again. Something whizzed past him on the road and he spun around sticking two fingers in the air at the stupid driver. Then, he thought for a moment, of his Hailey. What was she to him? Or more importantly, he to her? No more than a tease when all was said and done! When he thought of all he'd done for her and her family over the years. He paused and yelled across the busy road, 'She's a tease, they all are!'

His eyes seemed to blur and he wiped away the moisture that had filled them with his sleeve. What was it? Can't be tears, not from him. He stumbled again, his head confused. 'Men don't cry,' he said to himself. He turned around to complete his journey, but the verge had disappeared from his sight; all he could see was a stream of cars all heading for him. He couldn't quite figure out which way to go and froze in the middle of the road, just like a rabbit. He heard the screech of brakes and felt very little as he was catapulted into the air. He seemed almost to float in a silvery mist before landing hard on an unyielding ground, where an all encompassing blackness fell upon him.

★　★　★

David entered the office of 'Seekers', the detective agency he had hired to track his wife, following her every move.

'Mr Penwick. Good to see you again.' Mathew Blunt waited for David to sit down before he placed a buff coloured file in front of him on the desk. The file was very thin.

'Were you successful? Did you get the evidence so that, beyond all reasonable doubt, she is having an affair — or many?' David asked as he eagerly opened the file, but his smile dropped as he looked at the contents. He read list upon list and fumbled each page in turn, but there were no pictures. 'Well, have you revealed everything?'

'Absolutely, I can tell you definitely that after round the clock observation and extensive investigations your ex wife has not been having an affair with anyone. As far as we are concerned there is no evidence that she ever has. The baby must be yours after all, sir.'

Mr Blunt was obviously pleased with the thoroughness of his work.

'What!' David threw the paperwork back on the desk. 'You've missed something, you must have. What am I paying you for? Do you think I'm a fool? All those visits to that health club, she must be having an affair with the trainer or someone. You've missed something, or she knows you are watching her.'

'I can assure you, we haven't. For two months we've had people shadow her every waking hour. She takes extremely good care of herself and we cannot find any links to anyone within the last year. We have been extensive in our investigation. It is all detailed in our invoice.' Mr Blunt looked blankly at him.

'Don't worry you'll get your cheque, but you're wrong, you must be. I'll insist on a paternity test. She's not getting

195

away with this. I know she'd been cheating on me.' David slammed a fist against the desk. The idea that he had misread her was impossible — it was beyond his comprehension.

'We have no proof of that, and I'm afraid we can't help you further with the paternity suit. So if you wish us to conclude our investigation, we will have your account made up and finalised.' Mr Blunt looked sternly at him. He collected up the file and placed it inside a large manila envelope. He handed it to David. 'Mr Penwick, you'll find all the details in there. I should read it carefully before accusing her in court. There is no evidence to back up your claims and I can assure you, Mr Penwick, we have been thorough in our investigations.'

'Whatever! She must have realised you've been following her.' He snatched the envelope from the man and stormed out of the office. He almost knocked a woman off her feet as he left the building.

Sitting behind the wheel of his car he read through the details of the 'thorough' and comprehensive report on his ex wife; the 'ex' he had jealously and possessively accused of having affairs behind his back, throughout their turbulent marriage. Everything she had told him was the truth had been borne out by the words he now read. Had she been telling him the truth then, all along? David was dumbstruck. How could he have misjudged her so? No, she must have realised she was being watched. Surely he couldn't be wrong. He prided himself on knowing how other people think, it was how he stayed one step ahead. 'Shit!' he shouted and started the engine. 'What a damnable mess!' The child he had longed for in their marriage had arrived, but far too late and now he had a whole new future planned and another child.

He roared off down the road and was only snapped out of his anger and shock when a flashing light caught his attention. As he saw the box behind him flash he realised he'd just had three points added to his licence and a fine would be arriving in the next few weeks. He was numbed by the sudden turn in his life's fortunes, because that would be what it was going to cost him, an absolute fortune. Bringing up one child within wedlock and one outside of it, if, as it appeared it was his also, he'd face a financial drain that he just didn't need. Besides, he liked to be in control of things. How can he acknowledge and include the other child in his plan? — unless she'd let him adopt it. But then would Kate raise two? Oh, it was all so messy. He needed time out to think things through. David would decide upon the best course of action and solve the problem. It was what he was good at. He hadn't got far outside of the town when he was met by a gridlock of traffic.

'Kate,' David spoke into his mobile phone. It was such a comfort to him to hear her voice. She was a good girl; he could trust her because she was not as worldly wise as his first wife had been. She respected his maturity and he liked that.

'Yes, David.' Just hearing Kate's voice cheered him up a little bit.

'I'm stuck in a blasted traffic jam. The traffic's solid so I don't know when I'll be in,' David complained to her bitterly. Someone tapped on the car window. 'Just a minute, Pooch.'

'What is it?' he asked, as a lorry driver in a day glow jacket told him, 'You may as well switch off, mate. Some guy staggered out of the hotel into the road, pissed as a newt, and has caused a bit of a pile up. They've got to clear a jack-knifed lorry before anything can move. We'll be here for quite a while.' The man shrugged his shoulders and turned away. Obviously he had no idea how long the while would be.

David dropped the phone into his lap. 'Was anyone killed?' he shouted after him, as a huge knot formed in his stomach. He was thinking about Simon, realising which hotel it was that the man had meant.

'Well, there are a few cases of whiplash and such, and a couple of motors won't be fit to drive home tonight, but I don't think anyone died.'

'What about the guy who walked onto the road?' David shouted after the man, as he continued to move on to tell the next driver in the queue.

'Don't rightly know that. The bloody idiot was taken to the hospital soon as the ambulance arrived.' The man was then out of earshot, but David had no more questions he wanted to ask him.

'David! David what's happening?' Kate's panicky voice was shouting at him from the mobile in his lap.

David picked it up. 'Sorry, Poochy. Looks like I'll be here for a few hours. Look, there's a hotel just up here. If I can, I'll have dinner there and if it clears I might still be back by morning. I've got some stuff to work through anyway.'

'OK, but take care, David. Hailey is coming over here now. I'll speak to her;

if she's been holding out on me I've a right to know.' Kate sounded indignant.

'Kate, take it easy with her. Find out how she felt about this guy. Don't forget we didn't open up to her, did we?' David's voice was almost mellow.

'Well whose idea was that, David?' Kate asked, knowing the answer only too well.

'Mine, Kate, and perhaps it was not one of my better ones.' He stared blankly as another ambulance screamed past him.

'David, are you feeling all right?' Kate sounded really concerned.

'Yes, I'm fine, just tired,' David sighed, 'Kate.'

'Yes, David.'

'I do love you.' His voice was softer than usual.

'David?' There was a slight pause, but he gave no response, 'Yes, me too.'

'Bye.' He switched off his phone having heard the words he craved and made his way to the hotel.

13

Hailey arrived at Fenchurch Street station, purchased her ticket and sat on the cold steel bench waiting for the train to arrive. It would take her at least an hour to make her way to Kate and their home. She hated letting anyone down but James was right; there was time for her to take some space of her own before the baby arrived. Besides, Kate wanted to work until she was wheeled into the maternity ward, or that was how she presumed it would be. Text book stuff, but then it was her first and why shouldn't she believe it could be that way?

Hailey boarded the train and sat gazing out at a strange new world. Looking over at the Tower of London and then Canary Wharf as they passed by, she realised there was so much in the world she wanted to see. Her thoughts turned to James and she let her mind wander, imagining them both on a ferry, forgetting conveniently about Sarah, Simon, David or anyone else for that matter.

The journey soon passed and, a taxi drive later, she arrived at what was supposed to be her new home. But it wasn't and it would never be. Beautiful as it was, it would never be her choice of anything. Everything would have to fit in with Kate and David's aspirations and tastes as it should be, which made her realise that it was not for her. She rang the highly polished bell.

'Hailey, am I glad to see you!' Kate opened the door with a look of huge relief on her face. 'Where's all your baggage?' she asked, obviously surprised that she should arrive without it.

'James's looking after it for me,' Hailey answered brightly, realising this was not going to be easy.

'James is? Why James? What has he got to do with you coming here? David told me you had two old large suitcases with you,' Kate asked as Hailey walked in.

'Because,' Hailey took a deep breath, 'I asked James to look after them whilst I came to see you, to talk to you alone for once.' Hailey smiled cheerfully and then hugged her sister. 'So how's the little mum?'

'Really confused, Hailey and worried.' Kate looked at her sister and shrugged her shoulders dismissively. 'What on earth have you been up to Hailey? It's not like you to play games, you're usually boringly up-front.'

'Then let me explain. You see, Kate, I've thought long and hard about it, your proposal and your situation here and how I would fit in with it. It doesn't feel right, so I need some time to sort myself out.'

'Well time is one thing that will be limited and, if you decide you're going to say no, then I will have even less time to sort out my childcare,' Kate said and placed her hands firmly on her hips.

'Kate, can't you think beyond yourself

for once. This is my life too and you now have to think of a child before yourself. I think one problem of me being here is that you wouldn't.'

Kate opened her mouth to speak but Hailey put up her hand.

'No, I'm not being cruel, Kate, I'm being honest. If I was here you would end up leaving things to me. You trust me and in time I think you would resent it. That is why I'm taking six months out to help James with his new business idea and also to find out what I want to do about the mess I've created of my life. I suggest you use the time to think things through seriously as well.' Hailey gave her sister another hug. 'I have to sort myself out before I can help anyone else, Kate. You have a baby growing within you; it is going to need all your love and caring, first and foremost. Think about it.'

Kate moved away. At first she stared out of the window in silence, and then with dewy eyes she turned to her sister. 'I've never been so scared, Hailey, since

Mum died. I should be happy, in a way, I am, but the changes have all come together so quickly. I feel as though just as I have had choices given to me, they have all been taken away again.'

The two sisters sat down and talked to each other honestly and openly. Kate explained how she had met David and been completely swept up by him, his lifestyle and his love for her.

'I know he takes charge, Hailey. But I love my life with him. He does love me and he wants to look after me in a way Dad never did with Mum,' Kate explained. 'He will look after me, Hailey.'

Hailey thought about her sister's reply and could understand why Kate craved the security that David could provide her with.

'That's great, fantastic even, but I need my space too. I've not been honest with you over the years either. I made a mistake with Simon that I bitterly regret for both of our sakes, especially Paula. I thought it was over and done with but when you left he thought our time had come and he — well, he became persistent. Scary even. I ran, Kate, and I'm not proud of myself for doing it but I didn't want him to do something that would put him in trouble; and me — well, I couldn't handle him. So I'm here, but then James offered to give me some space and it is where I know I want to be, for now.' Hailey revealed to Kate the truth of what had happened between her and Simon and why she needed to sort herself out. James had given her the chance to do something completely different, and to be able to decide what she was going to do with her life before it was too late for all of them.

'James is a rat!' Kate said. 'He has an 'ex' and he might have a current. Do you want to be treated like Michelle was?' she asked.

'I didn't say we were an item. He is a friend I have just met, that is all. I don't rush in . . . '

'Where angels fear to tread?' Kate

raised her eyebrows at her as if she was having a personal jibe at her.

Hailey nodded. Both women embraced each other, both cried, but most importantly, both understood the other openly for the first time in years.

*   *   *

David managed to pull into the hotel and order a sandwich. He found out from the barman that it was, by his description, Simon who had staggered into the road. He also obtained the name of the hospital that he had been taken to.

*   *   *

Simon awoke. His head and body were in a painful blur. His head was bandaged and his body ached all over. He saw a drip at the side of his bed that was fed into his arm. Oh, how he hated needles, and hospitals. He felt as though he was completely encased by something hard. He tried to move and look down at the rest of his body, but he ached too much.

A figure entered the room — a female. 'Hailey?' he mouthed the word but no sound came out.

'Simon, what the hell were you doing?' The voice was familiar, but it was not Hailey's. 'You know how to give a girl a hell of a shock.'

The figure moved into focus and knelt by his bed. The tear-stained face of Paula appeared next to his own. 'Tell me what possessed you to walk out into the middle of a dual carriageway? Was it our split? You silly man, you could've got yourself and others killed.'

'Paula, I couldn't carry on, I lost me path. I just didn't know where I was going.' Simon was gradually realising he was in some sort of body brace.

'Simon, we all feel like that sometimes, but why didn't you come to me? You know I love you, and I always will. Don't you fret about a thing, Paula will see to it.' She gently stroked his forehead.

Simon realised she had completely misunderstood his meaning, but turned it to his advantage as she was showing such concern for him.

'We're bloody well divorced; that's how much you loved Simon.' A tear rolled down his cheek as the certainty hit him that he was not going to be up and walking within a week. He felt a surge of pity for himself, he was very scared.

'Look, lad, I had a fling, granted. And I know two wrongs don't make a right, but you only ever looked at that young lass next door. You talked about her as if she was a bloody angel. You didn't even seem to know I was there anymore. Simon, I never wanted Andy or anyone else, just you.' Paula sobbed and Simon strained his eyes to see the hurt in her face. 'I just wanted you to notice me and realise that I was also attractive to others like. All you did was get mad, and we couldn't talk anymore. I thought you didn't love me.'

'Paula, I'm sorry, Hailey needed my help. You know the situation she was left in. Lass, I'm frightened. Am I ever going to stand up again?' Simon asked, his face almost distraught.

'Yes, of course you are, but we're going to have to be very patient and take it slowly, like. You've hurt your back and they are going to keep that thing on whilst pins mend it.'

Simon's eyes widened and he paled at the thought . . . pins.

'Your daughter's coming to see you tonight.' She sniffed, and forced an artificial smile on her face.

'We, you said we?' Simon's voice broke with emotion.

'Yes, I said we. I never wanted to divorce you,' Paula admitted.

'I thought I loved her. Will you stay by me, Paula, even after all I've put you through?' Simon closed his eyes as he waited for her answer.

'Yes, love, even if it makes me the biggest fool on this earth.' She laughed, a nervous high laugh that echoed around the sparse room.

'No, no, lass, you're not the fool. Was

anyone badly hurt in the car crash?'

'Fortunately not, now rest.' She kissed his forehead and remained seated at his side whilst he slept.

★　★　★

David arrived at the hospital as Paula had popped out to get a drink from the vending machine. She heard him ask the receptionist about the man who had been in the accident. 'Simon somebody, his name was.'

'Are you a relative?' the receptionist asked.

'No, a friend,' he replied and for once the lie nearly stuck in his throat.

'Excuse me,' Paula answered, 'I'm his wife. Can I help you?' David turned to the woman who had been standing to the side of him. She was middle-aged, overweight, but quite smart.

'Yes, thank you.' David smiled at the receptionist and walked over to some plastic seats with Paula. He hated hospitals. They smelt and, to David, they represented the ugliness of life, the part he avoided. Now, he was here, and regretting the unusual stab of conscience that had driven him to find the place. After all, it was the hotel's fault for letting the guy loose in the state he was. He would take no responsibility for any of it.

'Who are you?' Paula asked and he could tell that she was far more astute than her fool of a husband, or her ex.

'I'm related to your neighbours, Hailey and Kate,' David said, and tried to sound as genuinely pleasant as he could. He had intended to find out if he still lived, or the state he was in, and then clear the place as fast as he could. He had had no intention of getting involved in any way. 'How is Simon?'

'Apart from a concussion, a cracked spine and numerous cuts and bruises, he's doing very well, considering. He's alive if that's what you wanted to know, though,' Paula said calmly and tilted her head slightly on one side as she spoke to him.

David realised he had made a big mistake.

'Of course I want to know he's alive and I'm very sorry he is so badly hurt. You must be very upset. I'll leave you to your privacy and return when he has had time to rest. Goodbye.' David stood up.

'Was that what you were going to do at the hotel, only you forgot to let him know, eh?' Paula stood up and although she was short she stared him down. He had little experience of feeling small.

'I don't know what you mean, Mrs?' David tried to look shocked.

'I saw you drive off with him from Hailey's place. I was at my friend's house across the road. He never drinks in posh hotels. He wasn't driving and he ain't got wings. The barman told the cops he'd been seen drinking with a bloke in a suit. You, I guess!' She prodded him with her finger. 'So what were you doing with my Simon and what possessed you to leave him stranded out there in a state?'

214

'Please keep your voice down, madam. This is a hospital,' the receptionist asked.

'Sorry,' Paula apologised but still glared at David.

'I only spoke to him, Mrs? I'm Kate's fiancé. He got a bit hot under the collar about Hailey. I had an appointment to go to in town and he needed to cool off. How was I to know he'd decide to walk home? I left him twenty pounds for a taxi. I'm not his nursemaid. If he chose to drink it instead, that is hardly my fault.' David was used to spinning lies or stretching the truth. This time it bothered him, but he would get out of this mess, and never ever return to the place, he was a survivor. He opened his wallet. 'Look, if he needs anything, take this . . . ' David pulled out two fifty-pound notes.

'Mister, if I wasn't a lady I'd tell you where to stick them. Get out of my sight and our lives and tell that Hailey to leave my man alone. When 'e's fixed, I'm keepin' him. Got it?' Paula was cerise.

'Got it!' Stunned, humiliated and relieved to be dismissed, David left her and returned to his car, swearing he would never visit this part of the country again. Like all things he'd put it behind him and move on.

* * *

James entered Blake's office. This time he was going to lay it on the table for Blake. There would be no fudging, and no going back and nothing he said to him would change his mind. 'I want to resign from my full-time position and offer my services on a client basis only, based from my new office on the Isle of Wight.'

Blake looked straight at him. 'You're a bloody fool, James. You're throwing away a chance to take over the London office. What you don't realise is that I am moving on to open an office in New York. This is your chance to take over here. You can fill my shoes, if you're big enough.' Blake looked back at his papers. 'Take another week's leave. Sort your head out and come back here and we'll talk about it then.' Blake swivelled his chair around; it was how he dismissed people.

James left. Run the London office? Fill his shoes? It was the man's head that was too big for James to compete with not his feet. He ran his hands through his hair as he took the elevator down to the ground floor. What the hell was he doing with his life? Where had his determination, his resolve, gone? He walked and walked until he found himself by the embankment staring at the Thames. His head was in a whirl, but one thing he was certain about — he wanted to be with Hailey. Together they'd work out their individual problems. He had one week and he intended they would both enjoy it to the full. James wanted to have some fun and relax in the company of sincere people.

★   ★   ★

David arrived back home, totally shattered and drawn. He'd driven through the night, his mind numbed by events. Simon could have killed himself and taken several people with him. He'd wanted to teach the wretch a lesson not cause mayhem. Then there was the other issue. How would he tell Kate that their child might have a legitimate half brother, or sister? How could he be father to both, unless his ex let him adopt it? Might be better in the long run. Then he'd have to persuade Kate to accept the other child as well as her own. Not that he sensed she was oozing with maternal hormones yet. Then he thought about Hailey. Well, she could look after two as easy as one, so he couldn't see that being a problem. After all, she had more experience in that sort of thing than Kate. By the time he reached home, he'd convinced himself that he would sort it all out to everyone's advantage. It would cost money though, but what the hell was it there for. No, he was sure that life would be sweet again.

'David, you look awful,' Kate said, as he came through the front doorway.

'Thanks, you look great, Pooch, as always.' He kissed her cheek and wrapped his arm around her shoulders.

'Hi, Hailey,' David acknowledged her as he sat down on a comfy chair.

'I'll get you a coffee.' Kate ran off to the kitchen.

'Enjoy your trip, David?' Hailey sounded sharper than she had intended to, and saw the surprised expression on his face.

'Not really.' David looked at her. 'I spoke to Simon. You are a dark horse, Hailey.'

'Hope you enjoyed the chat.' Hailey didn't give away any trace of emotion.

'He was waiting for you to return. He seemed to think you and he were an item . . . ' David watched her face as if monitoring her reactions.

'Well, we're not and have never been so he's in for a very long wait.' Hailey folded her arms defiantly.

'Oh, he's going to have to be a patient man that is for sure.' David did not explain his comment further as Kate returned.

'Did you tell him I'm not interested or has he ideas of chasing me down here?' Hailey asked as she had half-expected Simon to appear like a bad apparition, to haunt her.

'No, he's decided to stay put. In fact I think he is reuniting with his ex wife, Paula,' David added with no further explanation.

The relief in Hailey's face was blatant. 'Fantastic, I'll phone her later and . . . '

'Why not stay well out of their lives and let them find their way together again,' David offered her what sounded like good advice and, for once, Hailey could see the logic in his words.

Kate curled up next to him on the settee.

'David, Hailey and I have been talking to each other about things.' Kate winked at Hailey as David was reaching for his mug of coffee and looking the other way. 'We've decided that Hailey may as well use the next few months to have a complete break. After all, I'll be at work all day.'

'Where are you going to have a break for months?' David asked sarcastically.

'The Isle of Wight sounded like a nice place to stay for a while,' Hailey answered confidently, realising it would rock David's plans for once.

'And you want David to cough up for it?' He looked at Hailey smugly.

'Actually not. It will be a working holiday,' Hailey announced proudly. 'I'll pay for myself, I always have.'

The doorbell rang.

'I'll get it.' Hailey stood up.

'Who the hell will that be?' David asked.

'James,' Hailey answered and saw the look of surprise on David's face.

Hailey opened the door and, without saying a word, gave James a warm smile as she led him in. He grinned back then she sat next to him.

'This is my new boss.' Hailey looked up at James, who was still smiling, but something told Hailey he had a distant troubled look about him.

'What!' David nearly exploded. 'I offer you a position in my firm and you waltz off with my sister-in-law. What the hell do you think you're playing at?' Kate and Hailey exchanged worried glances. This isn't quite how they'd planned things going.

'David, you're tired.' Kate tried to get him to sit down again.

'To hell with tired. Get out of my house, Hood! And as for you,' he turned his attention towards Hailey, 'you had better get yourself settled. You've broken one man's heart already. Don't start your ways in here! You're no little Miss Innocent,' David exploded in an outburst of rage.

James got hold of Hailey's hand. 'Come on, we're leaving right now. Thanks for the offer, but no thanks, David. I've had much better ones, without the tantrums.'

'Hailey, if you go with him then don't think I'm going to let you live under my roof. It's your choice.' David pointed a warning finger at her.

'It always has been my choice, David. Goodbye, for now. Look after Kate, and your child.' Hailey winked back at Kate and left with James.

She had made her decision.

★ ★ ★

Paula arrived early at the hospital as usual and kissed Simon's forehead. She smoothed his sheets and calmed his mood. She had his undivided attention and saw to his every need.

'I did the right thing when I married you, lass,' Simon said in his dry crackle of a voice.

'I know, what about the divorce, though?' Paula asked.

'Oh, lass, we can forget it ever happened. Start over, eh?' Simon coughed slightly and then instantly grimaced.

'Do you really mean it?' Paula asked

223

again, obviously excited by the thought.

'Well of course we can. It will be better, though, this time — no distractions. Once I'm up and running again, you'll see a new Simon.' He smiled as she kissed his lips.

'Wait till I tell our lass. I'll speak to the hospital Chaplain and see how we arrange it.' Paula stood up and started to walk to the door.

'Chaplain? What? I thought you said I'd recover!' Simon's voice broke as he felt the panic rising in him.

'Silly sod, for the wedding arrangements, of course. The setting won't be as romantic as our original one, but under the circumstances it's still very romantic. Mind, we'll have to wait a while for the honeymoon.' Paula beamed at him, and then winked.

'You want us to have a service in here with me like this? Why not wait until I'm better and do it proper like.' Simon was desperate. He needed Paula. Without her who would look after him. She was the only one who was there and prepared to see to him, if he was ever going to be well again and talk to Hailey — reason with her. He needed Paula now.

'We have to seize the moment, love. Live for the day and all that. You do love your Paula, don't you?' She looked at him coyly and he knew he was totally lost. If he said no, she'd go and there would be no coming back. There was no way out. He needed her — and she'd always wanted him.

'Of course I do, pet.' Simon forced a smile. 'It's just I feel so awful and . . . '

'Good, I'll sort it all out. Don't you worry about a thing and our lass will be bridesmaid. You lay there and recover and I'll be back soon, lover.' Paula left with a bounce in her step that was unmistakable.

'Damn!' Simon lay there, trapped, defeated and contemplating his life in the hands of Paula. After this he'd be banned from cigarettes, alcohol and Hailey for life. What a life! But then at least it was one.

14

James and Hailey arrived back at his apartment after a quiet journey. Both appeared to be lost in their own thoughts of recent events. Hailey took in all the sights and could not help but look around in awe as he drove her through the city around St Paul's and onwards towards the embankment. It was a hectic and intriguing city with a vibrancy of its own. True it was dirty and chaotic in part but so different to her.

His apartment was as she imagined it, modern, yet homely and had a view over a small park square. In his hallway stood her two old cases; they looked so out of place here. James saw her looking at them.

'You don't need to take all that over to Wight with you. I can put them in my spare room whilst we visit Sarah, and you can decide what you wish to do.'

'Are you sure?' she asked. 'They don't exactly fit in with the decor,' she added and looked around her.

'I'm sure that they'll fit in neatly with my spare room. Look.' He crossed the hall and opened the door. A room, rather like a large cupboard was half filled with a collection of cardboard boxes; the opposite wall had coat hooks on which hung a collection of coats for all activities. 'See there's just room for them to slide down the middle.'

'Is that really classed as a room?' she asked inquisitively.

'Yes, this is London and space is a premium, so oversized cupboards do qualify as rooms, I'm afraid.'

There was an electronic sound, like a series of long mellow beeps. Hailey glanced at what looked like a control panel on the wall. James pressed a button and asked, 'Can I help you?'

'I hope so, lover. I need to recover my things. Any objections?' Michelle's voice, clear and shrill seemed amplified as it echoed around the silent room.

'Should I leave?' Hailey whispered to James.

'No,' he said back.

'Why not?' demanded the bodiless voice from the intercom. 'They're too small for you.'

He put a hand on Hailey's shoulder and squeezed it gently as if he was reassuring her that her presence was not a problem.

'Michelle, I wasn't referring to you. I have a friend with me here. Come up.' He released the button and walked Hailey over to the open kitchen at one side of the room. The wooden flooring gave the place a feel of space. The plain walls had a few colourful modern pictures decorating them, and the large window at the end provided the ample feeling of daylight to finish off the clean and appealing effect. Two terracotta coloured sofas were placed at right angles to each other around a rich coloured Turkish rug. As she sat on one of them, she noticed the flat plasma screen TV on the wall. 'Are you sure I won't be in the way, James?' she asked as the flat door bell rang.

'I wouldn't have asked you to stay if I thought you would be.' He gestured to her that she should stay seated when she stood up again. 'Relax,' he said as he passed her, 'You've been honest with me about your skeletons in your cupboard, now meet one of mine.' He smiled and walked towards the door. She tried to feel comfortable, but still felt ill at ease. Hailey remembered the spirited beauty who had thrown her wine over James in the Italian restaurant.

'Sorry to interrupt, James.' Michelle walked boldly into the flat as if it was her own. 'Ah, coffee, I love that smell.' She was every bit as beautiful as Hailey remembered her. Long blonde hair rested upon what looked to be a beautifully cut short jacket. She was tall, slim and confident. 'And you are?'

Hailey looked at Michelle as she

swung her leather bag off her shoulder and dropped it by the settee before collapsing onto the adjacent sofa.

James interrupted. 'Would you like to join us for a drink, Michelle, or are you in a hurry?'

The last part of the question could have been a hint or a hope, Hailey wasn't sure which, but either would have been lost on Michelle, who hugged a cushion and answered him sweetly, 'I'll always make time for you, James. A coffee would be great.'

James winked at Hailey before pouring out their drinks.

Michelle smiled at Hailey. 'Have we met before? There is something slightly familiar about you.'

'My name is Hailey and I . . . ' she glanced up at James as he handed her and Michelle their coffees.

'No, I don't think you have ever been introduced before, Michelle.' He collected his own drink and sat down cross legged on the rug.

'So Michelle, what did you forget

when you packed up last time?' James asked her calmly.

'I left some personal things in there.' She nodded to the bedroom door and casually glanced at Hailey as if trying to judge her reaction.

Hailey sipped her coffee, wishing she was a million miles away.

'So, Hailey, what do you do?'

Michelle reminded her of one of her friend's cats that would curl up on a chair opposite her and quietly purr with satisfaction; watching her, not missing one move. Hailey thought she liked the cat more than Michelle and that was not much at all. Before James could leap to her defence again, she calmly answered, 'I am between jobs at the moment, but will shortly be working with disadvantaged children.' Hailey liked the sound of that but could see that it did not appeal to Michelle. 'What do you do?' Hailey asked.

Michelle smiled confidently. 'I'm a model, dear.'

'Yesterday's' was the unkind thought

that flitted through Hailey's mind and she had to stifle the urge to grin, because the woman was so vain.

James finished his coffee. 'Come on, Michelle, we have to be going shortly, so let's get your stuff sorted.' He placed their cups on the counter, she held up her hand and he instinctively took it in his and led her to the bedroom. 'Just like old times,' she said as they entered the familiar room. Her words were spoken just loud enough for Hailey to hear them. She sipped nervously at her own drink, trying hard to resist the temptation to eavesdrop.

'No it isn't, Michelle. It will never be that way again.' James turned to face her and she instantly wrapped her arms around his neck and kissed him firmly on his lips. He was surprised by her action and for a minute found himself in her embrace but he peeled her off and stepped back leaning next to the door frame. 'Behave yourself, we were over a while ago but you wouldn't let go — do it now. Move on, Michelle.'

She opened a drawer and pulled out a few panties and put them in her bag. 'Actually, I have, James. I'm going to do some work in New York.'

James raised an eyebrow. 'You've hitched up with Blake?' he asked her but there was no need. It was written in the smug expression on her face.

She pushed past him. 'You see you weren't such a great catch. I found a bigger fish.' She looked at Hailey who was washing up the mugs. 'Looks like you've moved down the food chain to the cleaning lady. Hasn't she heard of dishwashers?' Michelle walked quickly to the door. 'Bye, Hailey, don't let him work you too hard.' She left.

'Sorry about that. She is a . . . '

'Bitch,' Hailey added the word to finish his sentence.

'Yes.' James ran his fingers through his hair. 'In fairness to her, though, it is I who changed, so in a way she has every right to feel angry.'

'People do.' Hailey wanted to be out of the flat; it represented his past and, like her own, would have no part of her future. 'So should we change now and set about on our new venture?'

He nodded his agreement. They both packed up a small bag and in no time were ready to set off again. Hailey wondered if his new 'friend' was far removed from the old one. The situation was awkward for her. She liked him very much and when he was close to her she felt as though the feelings were reciprocated, but she had to go to find out who this Sarah was and what she was to him. There was no way for her to go but forward.

15

Kate stared at David over the breakfast table. He looked pale to her, almost as pale as she did. The healthy, rosy glow of a pregnant woman had not quite settled upon her yet. Instead she started every day feeling tired, sickly and ill. She was used to having energy and that too had dipped. Was this how it was going to be for the next nine months? The thought depressed her. That was another thing which concerned her. Her moods just weren't her own anymore. One minute the future looked fine, glowing and content, whilst the next she was glum, disheartened and fearful. Of what she did not know, but it was that way.

'What happened up there, David?' She sipped her coffee and waited for him to glance over his paper at her. He had not spoken to her after James and

Hailey left the previous day. It was as though he was locked in his own private raging battle. He looked like a soul in torment. After much consideration she had decided that there had to be more to this than just annoyance that Hailey had altered his plans for her. She had tried to instigate a conversation, gently coaxing him out of his shell, but he would have none of it. David retreated into a mood she had not known existed. He had cut her out, almost as though he was impenetrable. Even if she had felt at all like it, she doubted anything that 'Poochy' could have done to cheer him up would have reached him. So she had backed off until the dark clouds that had hovered over him drifted away and the David she knew, and loved, returned to her. It had taken a long and lonely night. She had longed for him to come to bed, just to be there with her, but he had slept in his study. She did not want his passion — not just at the moment. She wanted his presence and comfort — that, she could cope with as she came to terms with the baby inside her.

'I told you, Simon is hooked on that sister of yours and doesn't want to let go; so much so that he drunk himself into a stupor and walked out onto a major road and in front of a truck.'

His eyes did not meet hers until he heard the gasp as she put her hand to her mouth. 'Is he alright?'

'Yes. Well, he will be. His wife Paula is looking after him. He'll be out of hospital soon.'

David returned to his paper.

'How badly was he injured?' Kate was shocked by the news. Simon had always been a part of her past — in a sense her extended family. She could not imagine how badly he must hurt and how miserable he would be feeling. When she had first thought about leaving, it was he who had given her so much support and encouragement. She thought he had seen her predicament clearly and given unbiased advice to take control of her life and leave. When he had told her that it would be easier for Hailey if the parting was swift and clean and that he would be there to help her adjust, she had believed him without question. But now she knew that he had had his own motives, and she had played along with them, unwittingly, like a fool.

'Why should you care about him?' He stared at her, the black clouds moving over again.

'I've known him all my life, David. Wouldn't you expect me to be concerned about him?'

'I've told you he'll be fine. If that sister of yours persists in messing up everybody's lives the way she does, what can you expect?' He folded his paper and stood up.

'It's hardly Hailey's fault, any of it. Simon has always liked his drink. If he had designs for a future with Hailey, then perhaps he should have mentioned it to her. His accident was not her doing, was it?' She stared at David, who merely shrugged his shoulders.

'Whatever, it still happened.'

'She raised me single-handedly and now needs to be free of all of us. David, she may not return here as our nanny, but she is my sister and will always be welcome as my family.' Kate saw the colour rise in his cheeks. He was checking his temper. It was the first time she had spoken out regarding their home, as if she had any rights to say who came and went. Mind, she would have trouble accepting James. Kate decided she would deal with that one if and when it arose. The night had been long and Kate had done a lot of thinking. She couldn't just dump her baby onto Hailey and pretend that she would feel about life the way she had felt before; it just would not be right. She was creating a new one, not just for her but for a new little life. Neither would she stand by and have David dictate to her what their future would be like. Was this how his first marriage had started? She wondered how much of what he had told her about his ex was actually true.

'Don't upset yourself, Poochy. It's not good for you; you need to take it easy. She may realise that here is where her home and loyalty is — or should be.' David's voice sounded smooth, mellow even, or was it just plainly patronising.

'Her loyalty has always been with me, David. But I never saw it that way. So I'm giving it back to her. I don't want a nurse-maid anymore. I want to make my own decisions. Now, if you'll excuse me I'll call her and explain about Simon.'

Kate was surprised when he suddenly stood in front of her and blocked her way to the door. 'Don't do that. Let it be. I'm sure she is so wrapped up with this idea of James's to give Simon a second thought. Now, come on or we'll be late.' He put his arm around her waist and guided her out through the doorway. Something was disturbing Kate but she could not put her finger on what it was. One thing was for sure, though; a call to Paula would sort it out. She'd wait her time and then she would speak to Hailey. Even if the guy had a crush on her, she had a right to know what had happened.

Kate picked up her bag and thought it would be best to change the subject. 'So did you get the evidence you needed on your ex?' At first she thought that he had not heard her. So once they were inside the car, she tried again. 'So how many has she been playing around with then?' She looked at him and saw a muscle twitch nervously by his temple.

'No one,' he cleared his throat, 'Not whilst they had been watching her, anyway.'

Kate felt greatly ill at ease. Her stomach was feeling unsettled anyway, but this piece of news was so totally unexpected. 'You said that the child was not yours. You always said she had had affairs, lots of them. That you had been cheated on and so when we met it was not wrong, it was . . . fate,' Kate could not believe her ears.

'Look, I know what I said! I thought she was. Now, she may have outwitted them — the detectives, I mean.' He glanced at her as they drove out onto the main road. 'The child may very well be mine and we may have to acknowledge it. I don't see her as the natural maternal type, though, so she may even be open to a suggestion. After all we can provide a far more stable future for a child here than she could and . . . '

'We already will be, so don't get any ideas on that score. I'm not going to bring up two, not when I've my own child here.' She tenderly patted her stomach as she spoke to him, and for the first time felt strangely aware that she felt protective towards it, in a way she would not have believed possible.

'Look, I didn't want to go into any of this now. Time will tell how this will work out. Obviously she will want me to be involved in its upbringing and I shall have to be. But there's no point in fretting about that now. First things first, Pooch.' He smiled at her, patted her knee and then switched on the radio. Their conversation had just ended.

Kate stared out of the window. The world was moving too fast for her. She had made rash decisions and found herself in a world far removed from the one she had been raised in. It was more comfortable, faster and broader, but before she had been free, now the walls on her world were closing in. She closed her eyes and rested her head against the seat. David patted her knee; it was reassuring. If he had wronged his ex with her, she would make sure he did not repeat his mistake in their marriage, because Poochy was starting to change, to grow up.

★   ★   ★

By the time they boarded the ferry, James and Hailey had chatted to each other about their pasts for two and a half hours. Far from being the suave city type he was now, James had grown up on a farm in Devon. It sounded ideal to Hailey and she was surprised when he said it was, as an only child, quite lonely. His parents had both died, as he was born to them when they were in their middle years as he put it. So although money had never been a problem to him, the sense of loneliness, of not having that essential family unit around him had.

16

Hailey loved the island within minutes of arriving there. The pace seemed so much more relaxed than on the mainland or in the big city. London was a fascinating place to visit, though, and she had promised herself a theatre trip and a few days browsing the vast museums when she had the opportunity. She knew Kate would find both boring as she loved it for the shops and fashions.

Being next to the sea again touched a part of her that was so near to her heart and her roots. She loved it. Every different motion and mood, and the fresh air it brought to the shore; an ever changing view, which she knew she would miss if she remained land-locked for too long. Yet, this small island offered both countryside and coast alike. James seemed very relaxed here also as he drove along the coast road and chatted animatedly about the ideas they — he and Sarah, that is — shared for this small venture. He had to pull the old James up short as he started scaling the idea up to a much wider view to expanding onto the mainland, and then laughed at his own folly, for it was the simplicity and uniqueness that would keep Green Gables special. She laughed as he shrugged his shoulders and admitted that old habits die hard.

All the while, in the back of her mind, Hailey wondered if she was big enough to join in with the idea and see James and Sarah working as a team without feeling at least some pangs of jealousy. She loved being in his company. He, the newly discovered James, was a person she warmed to with an increasing depth.

'Here we are.' James smiled broadly at her as they reached a pair of large iron gates. He made to unclip his seat belt, but she tapped his arm and hopped out before he could. Hailey opened the gates wide, and waited by the side of the drive whilst James drove his car inside. She closed them behind him and turned around to face the large Victorian house. She could see that Sarah was waiting with Billie on the garden lawn. The boy was sitting in his wheelchair, not an old cumbersome one like her mother's was but a light sporty model. He made straight for James as he alighted from the car.

Hailey's attention focussed on the lady with the shoulder-length blonde hair. She was slightly older than Hailey had expected her to be and a more buxom build but, as Hailey focussed on her as she neared, it was the woman's kind eyes and welcoming smile that left her with no doubt that this was Sarah. She was attractive despite her size. She oozed confidence and personality.

'James, you made good time, I haven't even put the dinner on yet.' Sarah and James exchanged a brief hug. It made Hailey feel quite ill at ease. But she was suddenly aware that she too was being observed.

'Who are you?' Billie asked.

'My name is Hailey.' She looked down at the inquisitive face with the cheeky glint in his eye.

James swiftly intervened. 'This is my friend Hailey, who is about to become another friend of Green Gables, or at least I hope she will be.'

Sarah instantly held out a welcoming hand. 'Pleased to meet you, Hailey. Would you like a cup of tea?'

'That sounds like a good idea, but could you make it a coffee?' Hailey thought of her encounters and cuppa's with Simon. She had recently converted to coffee.

'So long as you don't mind decaff, I can,' Sarah replied, as she led the way into the house.

'Fine with me,' Hailey answered as James and Sarah started talking about how the work was progressing. It seemed to be doing well, but it was the atmosphere and size of the place that impressed her.

After a drink and a quick tour of the place, Hailey could see all their plans coming into fruition in her own mind. They seemed to be the perfect team; Sarah, amazingly practical and a natural manager with buckets of personality, and James the marketing man and financier. So it was with some feelings of guilt and sadness that she had to bury the first tinges of jealousy that emerged, deep within her heart. She did not want to be the hired help to a man she was falling ever more in love with, whilst watching him form the perfect working relationship with another woman — no matter how lovely she may be. Yet, when she chatted and played with Billie, she found it so easy to relate to him that she could not help but want to become involved in everything they were trying to do together.

Hailey was also aware that here was something useful she could do with her life and yet still have one of her own in a beautiful place and with a true purpose. Moreover, it touched a part of her deeply. She understood what it was to be handicapped and the levels of care that were needed, and all her life skills that she had learned in tending to and supporting her mother could now be applied to good use. Hailey retired early and prayed that night. In the morning she had made yet another life-changing decision. She would stay and help, but her own desires would be contained, at least until the place was up and running. If James and Sarah had been brought together then she must be happy for them as she had been guided here to help them set up the home. She had found her space and in time she was sure she would find much more.

The next few days were spent in a mixture of work, play and sightseeing. Those days turned into a week and that was when James asked her to go for a walk with him along Puckpool beach. The tide was out, a vast expanse of beach revealed, and the sun was high in the sky. They ambled along contentedly chatting about their short time on the island.

'You like it here don't you, Hailey?' he asked.

'Yes, very much so, and I can tell that you do. You are so much more relaxed around Billie and Sarah than you were in your suit listening to David.'

'Anyone would be more relaxed with them rather than with David. They are far less demanding . . . and honest.' He looked around him and then settled his eyes on her. He carelessly flicked a hair from her face. 'Hailey, will you be happy to stay here and help Sarah whilst I sort out a few problems in the city? I shall be gone about ten days, but then I hope to return here for another week or two.'

'I could come back with you and go and visit Kate. You know, smooth the feathers again.' Hailey was surprised at her own reply. It was automatic, yet, dishonest because she really only wanted to leave with him.

'Old habits die hard, don't they?' he

said as he looked down at her. How she wanted to hug him there, tilt her head to his and kiss his cheeks.

She nodded. It seemed the best response to let him think that she was thinking of others again, when in fact her motive was purely selfish.

He placed a hand on her shoulder, and she instinctively rubbed her cheek against it.

'Stay here, have some true space and get to know Sarah and Billie properly. Then when I return I shall be able to see things more clearly . . . we both shall. I have loose ends to tie up and you need to know how you adapt to life here.'

'Put like that, how can I refuse? However, I shall phone Kate and let her know my number because she is my expectant sister.' Hailey looked into his deep eyes and wished she could read what hidden thoughts lingered there as he stared back at her, lost momentarily in his own world.

'James?' she stroked his cheek.

'Sorry . . . I . . . Look, Hailey, I need

to speak to you when I return, but for now we have too many issues to sort out.' He dropped his hand down to hers and they walked on. She wanted to ask him what Sarah meant to him, but she was so reluctant to destroy the moment, and something told her that he was also not quite sure what he wanted either. So reluctantly they agreed to part, with a promise to continue their conversation on his return.

Hailey awoke the next morning to the sound of a car pulling away from the house. James had gone. Feeling strangely alone — deserted, she dressed and decided to seize the day. Her future was in the hands of God.

'Hailey!' Sarah shouted up the stairs as she appeared at the top.

'I'm just coming down, Sarah,' she answered.

'Oh, that's alright, ducks. There's a lady on the phone for you.'

'For me? Is it Kate?' Hailey asked as she approached the hall table where the phone was.

'She said something about needing to talk to you, didn't give her name, she said, love.'

Hailey smiled. 'That's Kate, my sister.'

'Hi, Kate, everything fine?' Hailey asked trying to sound cheerful.

'No it isn't, that's why I'm calling you!'

Hailey listened, thinking how some things never change.

17

Hailey and Sarah took Billie for a walk by the sea front, or to be more accurate, it was he who took them. He was extremely confident as he manoeuvred his wheelchair up and down the kerbs and around any obstacle that appeared in his path. Eventually he went off at his own speed and the two women were left to walk along together. It had been a fascinating experience and a lot of hard work, as rooms were prepared at the Gables. Builders came and went and the three of them had worked and played together as a team. Billie's natural energy and determination to be a full participant in life, was inspirational, it put them to shame so they stopped complaining and got on with the things that needed doing.

'I think James will be pleased with our progress when he returns,' Sarah commented. 'We're almost ready to start advertising the place and recruiting some part-time help. I don't know how I'd have hung on to the house if God hadn't placed him in our path when he did.'

'You have to be careful talking like that nowadays.' Hailey knew she sounded cynical, but she was so aware that to talk openly of her faith, in faith, had almost become politically incorrect; yet, she agreed wholeheartedly with what Sarah believed to be true. 'Faith isn't fashionable anymore; people like to feel they are in control of their own life.'

'Well, I don't care a hoot for fashion, and neither do you.' She smiled at her and then casually asked, 'So what will you do when James returns?' Sarah was looking at her with more than just an inquisitive glint in her eye.

Over the last few days, they had mentioned him in conversation, but had stopped short of crossing a more personal line. Sarah was definitely fond of him, but how fond she was unsure;

Hailey could not second guess that.

'Do you mean will I stay here?' Hailey asked innocently.

'Sort of,' Sarah answered and tilted her head on one side.

'I don't know for sure. I would like to but I need to work, I can't stay on an extended holiday for good, even if it is a marvellous place,' Hailey answered honestly, for although James had mentioned working there, until he returned, she had no idea what he meant.

'I'm sure James has a place ready to offer you if you are willing.' Sarah appeared to be quite amused, almost as though there were a joke that she was not a party to. Hailey decided to stop beating around the bush and ask Sarah straight, what her relationship with James was, but then if she did, she might jeopardise their friendship if she appeared to be competing in some way for him.

'Sarah, are you and James . . . ?'

'Hey, who wants an ice-cream?' Billie

came wheeling up at speed.

'Billie, when James bought you that chair it was with a clear health warning that you treat it and the general public with respect. So stop showing off and yes, I'd love an ice-cream.' Sarah looked at Hailey as she pulled out her purse. 'Sorry, love, you were saying?'

'Nothing important.' Hailey smiled broadly at them both, '99s okay?'

'Yes,' was the unanimous reply.

The day passed by, happily and easily as all the others had, but Hailey noticed that when they returned to Green Gables, Sarah's mood changed from light and bouncy; she was thoughtful and pensive. When Hailey approached her in the kitchen she was evasive. So she had no choice but to leave her alone, until she wanted to talk to her.

The opportunity came sooner than she had expected, once Billie had gone to his room. Hailey needed a pen so she went to Sarah's little study. It was a small room that literally had space for two chairs, a desk and an old filing cabinet. But Sarah had managed to make it cosy and very much hers.

'Are you OK?' Hailey asked.

'Yes I was just looking for something when I found George's death certificate. I miss him so much. It just came as a bolt out of the blue. The thing is that since I lost Georgie, life has never seemed so full of promise, until James appeared and put me back on track.' Sarah folded the paper back up, and placed it in a plain brown envelope.

'Georgie?' Hailey asked as Sarah had not mentioned him to her before.

'Yes, Billie's father. We were to marry and open this place together. He died leaving me and Billie in a bit of a pickle. Then, much later, James rescued us just as I was reaching the end of my finances and tether, and Billie looks so happy now. I don't want anything to ruin it all. It's not for me, it's for him. He deserves some happiness in this world too.' Sarah squeezed Hailey's hand. They looked into each other's eyes and both women understood the other.

'No wonder you love him so much,' Hailey's thoughts slipped out into words without her intending them too.

'Love him? I couldn't love him more if he were my own child. No, I really couldn't,' she answered with a heartfelt expression of motherly concern, but then as she saw Hailey's expression change she realised that Hailey hadn't been referring to Billie. A smile crossed Sarah's face, and the heaviness that had overcome her watery eyes, lifted until they too shone with humour. 'You meant James, didn't you?'

Hailey flushed slightly. 'Well . . . I . . .' She thought about lying, or stretching the truth, but saw how Sarah had seen straight through her veil. 'Yes, I did. I don't want to be in the way.'

'You foolish girl.' Sarah laughed and Hailey felt slightly put out as those were the very words she had used to describe Kate. 'Did you think that I would be interested in James? Don't get me wrong, I mean, he is handsome and a great catch but he's not my Georgie and never could be. No, I'm not his type, nor me his. You go for him, lass, before some city girl hooks him. He's a rare breed, a true gent.'

Hailey smiled. 'He may have his sights set higher than me, Sarah.'

'No, lass, I don't think so or he needs the opticians if he does. Believe me he sees you well enough. Now when he arrives tomorrow I'll keep Billie busy here and you get yourself down to meet that ferry boat and you tell him just how much you've missed him.'

Hailey gave her a squeeze. 'You believe things will be well. Take it a step at a time.'

'There's no other way. Now go and pour us out a nightcap.'

After Hailey had gone to bed, Sarah looked in on Billie, who looked as though he was fast asleep. She was about to close the door when he spoke to her. 'Sarah, can I call you Mum now?'

She was completely taken aback. She had prayed that one day he might consider telling her that she was like a mum to him, but had never thought he would utter the actual word to her.

'Of course you can, but what has brought this on all of a sudden . . . ' she looked back out of the door and along the hall towards her small office. The wheelchair was not folded up but placed next to the bed. 'You were listening to me and Hailey talking to each other weren't you?'

'I wanted to get some water. You'll be fine . . . Mum, honest. We both will, it's for you too you know.' Billie raised himself so that she could see him clearly. The same energy, determination and commitment filled his face as always.

Sarah walked over to the side of his bed. She fondly stroked his head and soothed his brow. 'I think so.' Bending low she kissed his cheek.

'Okay, don't go getting all sloppy, though.'

She chuckled and opened the door.

'I'm sorry about James.' His voice

drifted across to her full of an understanding beyond his young years.

'Yeh, me too, but you can't have everything in this world that you'd like and I was already blessed with the love of your father.' Sarah swallowed in the darkness.

'He wouldn't mind you know,' Billie added.

'Mind what?' Sarah asked, wondering if he was referring to Georgie or James.

'Dad. He'd want you to be happy, if you want James. He's a nice guy.'

'Yes, and both you and I know that Hailey is more than a match for him, so let's not get in their way, eh? There's been enough tears shed over the last few years, so no need to complicate things for people and make more. We've got each other.'

'Goodnight, Mum.'
'Goodnight, Billie.'

18

Hailey rose early and headed off to the Red Funnel ferry terminal waiting for the tell tale sign of the boat to appear on the horizon. She mulled over all the things that had happened and the many changes in her life. Kate had filled her in on everything that had occurred between Simon and David. Paula and her sister had discussed it at length and Kate had insisted that Hailey stay well away from him and Paula in the future. Hailey was more than willing to oblige her with this as any further interference on her part could only make matters worse. She cast off all feelings of guilt and felt free of the whole affair. It was as though a string that pulled her ever backwards and kept her in situ had been released, allowing her wings to unfold ready for her life to take flight. It was an awesome sensation and she thanked God for it.

Finally, the ferry appeared within her sight and her heart began to beat a little faster. She had missed him, she was in no doubt that she wanted him, and for once in her life she felt worthy of being loved by someone special. When James appeared in his car she stood at the junction of the car park and the road and waited to see the expression on his face as he saw her. It would be a deciding moment as it would tell her what she needed to know. He recognised her and instantly his face lit up. He stopped long enough for her to jump in and greeted her with a quick kiss on the cheek.

'Hello stranger, I was hoping you'd be here . . . alone.' He had to drive off or he would cause a traffic jam. James pulled away and headed straight for the coast road and the first available parking space that was sufficiently away from people to give them a little privacy. He said very little as they drove along. Once they were parked, he walked around to the passenger door and opened it for her offering her his hand, and she took it willingly as she stepped up beside him.

He led her up over the sea wall and onto the open beach. They hugged each other for a moment, it naturally became an embrace. Before a word was said they instinctively kissed each other, first gently, then with a growing enthusiasm and passion. Hailey felt light-hearted as she melted into his arms. She had never experienced such sweet blissful sensations before. James was so right for her. There was no need for words or promises. They had an understanding that was complete in itself.

As their lips parted once more she looked away, not knowing what to say to him. She didn't want this moment to end, or them to spoil it with words. Hailey felt confused as she didn't want them to meet Sarah, not just yet. She knew James thought so highly of her.

She had imagined that Sarah would be like another Michelle and that someone as good looking and stylish as James must have a Michelle in every port, yet, here he was loving her. It seemed surreal, too good to be true. Was that just a normal kiss to him, she wondered, but then dismissed the idea as his eyes told her everything she needed to know.

'What are you thinking about, Hailey?' he whispered into her ear, his breath almost teasing her as she felt it against her skin.

'Just thoughts, nothing really,' her answer was unconvincing and evasive.

'Tell me honestly, and no running away from them. What thoughts are flitting through that lovely head of yours? No hiding, not from me, I want you to share the truth.' He turned her around to face him and she looked up into his dark brown eyes.

She shared her doubts and fears with an open heart, questioning his feelings for her. She was honest about her own insecurity about her past, her looks and her desire to stay on at Green Gables

— but not without him, and then when she'd finished, she blushed.

He held her to him so tightly she almost gasped. 'You're a true wonder.' He followed the action with such a passionate kiss that she was breathless when they separated again. 'I don't have 'a thing' for Sarah. She's like the perfect sister, the one I always wanted but never had. You're beautiful, Hailey, and you can't see it, and that is the most attractive thing about you. You're more of a woman than Michelle can ever be; in fact you're a more rounded person in every way. I'm flattered that you feel this way for me too. I've been as fickle and greedy as the next man, but you fulfil something far deeper in me than I've ever known before and that is why I want us to be together, stay together, live together, here and in London. For a while we shall need two bases, but beyond that we can decide as a future unfolds.'

'We hardly know each other, James,' Hailey answered. 'Are you sure about this? It could be a reaction — a rebound.'

'Well, I'm too young for a mid-life crisis, I think, but a bit old to be growing up and that is what is happening to me. At last I have my priorities in the correct order and from now on you are to be my number one.'

'With Billie, Sarah, and . . . '

'Of course, they are an important part of my life now. Hailey, marry me? No more doubts, no more insecurity. Be the person you want to be with me.' He kissed her again, and again.

'Till death us do part . . . ?' she asked. 'Even though you haven't had a chance to like, love me properly or go off me yet, James?' Hailey persisted.

'Forever and ever . . . ' he kissed her cheek. 'Trust and faith, my darling. Without them we are nothing.'

'You don't know what you're saying. I think you had better not say anything else until the end of the week. Give yourself time to be sure,' Hailey insisted. But he growled low in his throat, mocking anger and frustration.

'Hailey!' he held her face in his hands.

'Yes, James?' She looked into his dark eyes.

'Just say, yes, and be quiet.'

'Yes, James.'

He kissed her and all her doubts disappeared. He slipped out of their embrace, going down on one knee in the middle of the open flat sands.

'Marry me, Hailey?'

She looked into his happy eyes and smiled back. 'Yes, James.'

They hugged each other until a small ripple of a wave lapped at their feet and like children they ran to the soft sand, enjoying the moment as it happened.

'Do you think Sarah and Billie will be surprised?' James asked.

'Somehow, I don't think so,' Hailey answered. He hugged her quickly before they climbed back into the car. 'Let's share our good news with our friends.'

They moved off along a straight road with a clear view of where they were both going and Hailey for once in her life felt as though she had a future, she had at last found the place she wanted to be in the present, and the person to share it with in James.

THE END

We do hope that you have enjoyed reading this large print book.

Did you know that all of our titles are available for purchase?

We publish a wide range of high quality large print books including:
Romances, Mysteries, Classics
General Fiction
Non Fiction and Westerns

Special interest titles available in large print are:
The Little Oxford Dictionary
Music Book, Song Book
Hymn Book, Service Book

Also available from us courtesy of Oxford University Press:
Young Readers' Dictionary
(large print edition)
Young Readers' Thesaurus
(large print edition)

For further information or a free brochure, please contact us at:
Ulverscroft Large Print Books Ltd.,
The Green, Bradgate Road, Anstey,
Leicester, LE7 7FU, England.
Tel: (00 44) **0116 236 4325**
Fax: (00 44) **0116 234 0205**

Other titles in the
Linford Romance Library:

VENTURE INTO DESTINY

Catherine Grant

When Melanie Crighton started her new job as companion to Chloe, Jake Masters' young daughter, it wasn't long before employer and worker became strongly attracted to each other. But this love affair could have no happy ending. Jake's magnetic personality ensured that he had an endless supply of admirers in his life, and Melanie feared that she was to be only one of his many 'affairs'. There was also the problem of his elusive wife Marion to consider . . .

THE ENDURING FLAME

Denise Robins

Inside his log cabin, in the Great White Wilderness, young Joanna Grey's father dies, and she's forced to flee from the lecherous Conrad Owen into the icy wilderness. Lost and exhausted, she's found by Richard Strange and they shelter in a cabin where they become trapped by raging snowstorms. And, despite discovering their love for one another, they agree that John should return to his wife. But then, terrifyingly for Joanna alone in the arctic night, Conrad Owen appears . . .